PENGUIN BOOKS

sparring with shadows

David Martinesi is a first-generation Italian Australian growing up in an inner-city suburb. He is fighting the shadows cast by his Italian upbringing, and this summer he is quietly waiting for change.

Change comes when David is befriended by confident, street-wise Nathan. But tragedy comes too . . .

sparring with shadows

with shadows

ARCHIMEDE FUSILLO

PENGUIN BOOKS

The author gives special thanks to his editors, Suzanne Wilson
and Karin Riederer, for their guidance and patience.

Puffin Books
Penguin Books Australia Ltd
487 Maroondah Highway, PO Box 257
Ringwood, Victoria 3134, Australia
Penguin Books Ltd
Harmondsworth, Middlesex, England
Viking Penguin, A Division of Penguin Books USA Inc.
375 Hudson Street, New York, New York 10014, USA
Penguin Books Canada Limited
10 Alcorn Avenue, Toronto, Ontario, Canada M4V 3B2
Penguin Books (N.Z.) Ltd
Cnr Rosedale and Airborne Roads, Albany, New Zealand

First published by Penguin Books Australia, 1997
10 9 8 7 6 5 4 3 2
Copyright © Archimede Fusillo, 1997

Designed by Glenn Thomas, Penguin Design Studio
Typeset in 11/14 pt Giovanni by Midland Typesetters, Maryborough, Victoria
Made and printed in Australia by Australian Print Group, Maryborough Victoria

National Library of Australia
Cataloguing-in-Publication data:

Fusillo, Archimede.
  Sparring with shadows

  ISBN 0 14 038656 4

  I. Title.

A823.3

To Alyssa, Laurence and Pina,
to finally know yourself is to be set free

Also for the family and friends who enrich my life

1

We were, I guess, about one-third of the way up the silo when my knees and elbows locked.

'Move your arse, Martinesi,' Nathan called into my ankles.

'I'm gonna be late home. Might be a better idea if we do this tomorrow.'

There was a moment of complete silence. I thought Nathan must have taken pity on me, then he came out with, 'Your dick's swollen, Martinesi.'

When I looked down I saw that Nathan Welsh was peering up under my footy shorts. As he laughed himself stupid I shuddered with embarrassment.

'You always get a hard-on when you're shit scared?' he taunted.

'I'm not shit scared,' I said, but there was no conviction in my voice.

'Well, we'll soon know won't we.' Nathan Welsh had a way of lowering his voice and talking almost in a whisper when he was pissed off. His voice was barely audible now.

'Listen, Martinesi,' he hissed through clenched teeth. 'Either you keep climbing or you jump, because I'm not climbing down just so you can chicken out.' Nathan wrapped both arms round the rung of the ladder and leaned hard into it.

We were both fifteen, Nathan four months older than me. Yet where I was stumpy and baby-fat soft, Nathan Welsh was built like an armoured tank. He had a thick neck and solid, squarish shoulders, and legs my mother would probably have said were like quality cured hams.

'I've got to give my dad a hand with the barbecue we're having tonight,' I tried. 'By the time we get all the way up, I'll never make it home in time.'

But Nathan was faking sleep, snoring loudly, ignoring my lame excuse.

'You're a shithead, Welsh, a real shithead,' I mouthed mutely.

'Huh?'

'Forget it.'

The silos were at the back of the house I lived in with my mum and dad, Teresa and Marco Martinesi, and my sister, Rose. I'd always wondered what the view from the top of those silos was like. From my back yard I'd often watched workmen scurrying along the narrow catwalks.

'You really should see someone about your dick, Martinesi,' Nathan mocked as we continued our climb. 'I mean, it just isn't natural for a guy your age to get a stiff over a piece of steel, you know.'

I only half-listened to the rest of Nathan's comments. I climbed slowly, one hand or foot at a time. I could feel the breeze on the cold sweat that had broken out along my spine. Now and then I'd pause and ask myself why, oh why I'd let Nathan Welsh talk me into doing what I was doing.

Of course I knew the answer: I had no choice. If I didn't

climb the silos I'd be back amongst the other stay-at-homes at school.

St Joseph's Catholic Boys College wasn't much different from any other school, and that meant that the coolest, most popular kids were the ones who were best at sport. A go-nowhere, pudgy, intellectual Italian guy like me was at the bottom of the heap, along with the other 'stay-at-homes', those that didn't play sport and anybody ethnic. Just above us came the bookworms. It was my life's ambition to get off the bottom of the heap.

Nathan Welsh was at the top of our year's hierarchy. Champion full-forward with the school football team. Four times best-and-fairest with the Collingwood District Under-16s. Under-15 high-jump champion. Nathan Welsh was the only student who could sabotage a major Science prac and not be suspended.

'You see, Martinesi,' Nathan told me once at school, 'you can be as bright as all fuck, but if you can't help Brother Ignatius win a premiership then you're no use. I mean, some of you intellectual types might end up as doctors or scientists, but by then poor old Brother Ig may not be around to bask in your glory. You get my drift?'

I got Nathan's drift.

Climbing the summit of the silos was a typical Nathan test for me being pulled up from the bottom tier. It was a dare. I had to fulfil it – or else.

Nathan often said us wogs were a pretty useless lot. We didn't even have any idea what holidays were about. According to Nathan, wog parents thought holidays meant time to repaint the guttering, mend the chook house, or add another slab or four of concrete to the back yard. The problem was that Nathan was right. One time though, when Nathan was leading the usual attack about this at school, I had seen my chance of shedding my tag of stay-at-home, and told him about my family's idea of a trip to Phillip Island with one of Mum's work friends.

'You don't even know where Phillip Island is!' Nathan had taunted. 'Your old man's probably already got the paint and brushes ready for the assault on the house.'

The other kids had laughed. After all, I was David Angelo Martinesi, and it was a well-known fact that I didn't go on real holidays.

'Why don't you try asking me a few questions about Phillip Island then, if you reckon I'm so ignorant about it?' The instant I had issued the challenge the mood around me changed. Voices were hushed, and those who'd been riding on my shoulders became shadows at my back. Nathan drew back a fraction, his eyes pin-pointed and his lips pursed into a tight thin scratch of a line across his face.

I knew what I'd done straight away. I had shown Nathan Welsh up. He knew even less about the island than I did. And even if he did know a whole heap about Phillip Island, who was I to demand he explain himself? What I should have done was laugh at his snide remark about my dad, the way we stay-at-homes always laughed off our humiliation.

Nathan Welsh had stood perfectly still, hands at his side.

I had never felt so sick in my life. My epitaph would read: Here lies David Angelo Martinesi, put out of his misery in one blow for having been a dickhead.

Without warning, Nathan Welsh had short-jabbed me in the groin, a punch so deft it had buckled me over and brought tears to my eyes.

Later that same day Nathan's note had arrived in my hand, courtesy of one of his Year 7 hangers-on: You're a stay-at-home until I decide otherwise, holiday or no holiday. Count yourself lucky I didn't smash your face into a vomit.

Saturday morning, ten sharp, be out the back of your house. It'll be just you and me. If you don't show, don't bother coming to school next year. And watch out 'cos I'll be at Phillip Island too.

How could I have refused such an invitation?

From the top of the silo I could look down and see Nathan's head, a mess of loose red curls like you'd see in a Rocky Horror nightmare.

'Where're we going?' I asked as Nathan hauled himself up beside me. He didn't answer and I had to pick my way after him, pretty sure that every step would be my last.

The view from the top of the silo was spectacular. It was *almost* worth the fear of plummeting to my death.

To the south were Melbourne's city skyline, the Exhibition Building with its distinctive dome, a puzzle of roads, laneways, side streets, and the mysterious Housing Commission flats.

Nathan ran along the decking, leaping across the narrow platforms between silos. I crawled along behind him, my hands vice-like on the handrails. The worst part was crossing between the platforms. One slip, I kept reminding myself, and my family would be burying an imprint.

'Hold these,' Nathan barked once we reached the centre silo. He held out a handful of loose change, a small red-handled pocket knife and a set of house keys. He was standing between platforms, one foot either side. The breeze ruffled his hair and he suddenly lost his grin, his face stern, concentrated.

'What're you doing?'

'Shh . . . Just stand there and shut up.'

I swallowed hard. We were a long way up. I felt my groin tighten and I swallowed hard again. I couldn't believe where I was. I was standing on the catwalk above the silos. Me – David Angelo Martinesi! I could look down into my own back yard. I could see my father's vegetable patch with the neat furrows into which I'd helped him empty seven sacks of chicken manure just last weekend. There was our weatherboard and tin garage, its flat roof slightly buckled. I could see how our fig tree grew up and over our garage and dropped its best fruit into the gutter. No wonder Dad always found the best figs; he knew where to look.

They lay below me. Rows and rows of houses, ramshackle back yards, clothes hoists heavy with washing, television aerials and the constant line of power poles. And in my parents' back yard garlic bulbs, onion stalks and chamomile stems hung out to dry. I could just see me in Mum's plastic apron, Dad's old workboots and a hairnet, prancing around helping to decapitate one of Mum's freshly bought chooks. What a sight! God, how often had Nathan Welsh been up here on a Saturday, looking down at us?

Nathan! I looked round at where he'd been standing, but he wasn't anywhere along the decking.

'Nathan?' Something cold and hard and weepy rose in my chest.

'Nathan?'

Nothing.

I glanced at my hand and Nathan's belongings, and suddenly it struck me.

Nathan had jumped! He had handed me his last few personal belongings and leapt to his death! I shivered, staggered backwards and almost lost my balance.

But why me? Of all the people to force up here alongside him, why me? What had I ever done?

Of course! How stupid of me. I'd made Nathan lose face in front of everyone. Me, David Angelo Martinesi, the kid who'd never been in a fight, never been kept in, never been sent to the office, never been on holidays. Me, the stay-at-home who stripped down to his Y-fronts to help his dad stomp the grapes for the wine. I'd pushed Nathan Welsh to commit suicide because I'd opened my mouth at the wrong time in the wrong place.

I had to get down, run for help. I had to find Nathan, or whatever was left of him. I shut my eyes against the thought of what I'd find at the foot of the silo.

I had to get down. I kept telling myself that. I had to get help. But still I kept my eyes shut. My head was spinning, and while I waited for it to stop I listened to the voice of the Higher Judge my Nonna said would one day banish all sinners to Hell.

'Mar-ti-ne-si . . . Mar-ti-ne-si . . . I am the spirit of Nathan Welsh. I've come back to haunt you . . .'

The too sudden sound caught me off guard and I dropped Nathan's money, pocket-knife and keys. I watched them fall as if in slow motion into an air vent that opened into the silo below. My eyes filled to bursting with terror and disbelief.

'You stupid wog fuckwit, Martinesi.' Nathan's voice split my thoughts. 'You stupid wog fuckwit. You've dropped my stuff!'

I jumped sideways, caught the hem of my brand-new shorts on the head of a bolt and ripped them.

Today, I told myself, is my day to die.

The footy shorts – not home-made for a change – were less than a week old, bought by my mum only after months of me begging and haggling and praying. At that moment I would have given anything to have been bashed black and blue by Nathan rather than face the wrath of a Martinesi woman, my mother.

'You dropped my gear,' Nathan repeated. He pulled himself onto the platform and stood staring at me as though I were some alien life force. 'I don't believe it, you actually dropped my stuff . . . You've dropped my stuff . . . I hope you're going to work out how to get it all back.'

Get it back? Was he kidding? He *was* kidding, wasn't he?

Just then a blur of movement to Nathan's left caught my eye. At first I thought it was a pigeon. I must have shown surprise or something because Nathan looked round too.

'RALPH!' he called. 'RALPH, DON'T BE STUPID.'

Suddenly Nathan disappeared again. Only this time I saw that just below me there was a kind of lower deck, much narrower than the one I was on. And this deck opened up to a kind of sheltered, obscured part around the neck of the silo. This must have been where Nathan had gone when I thought he'd jumped to his death.

'Ralph,' Nathan was saying, his voice lowered, 'Ralph, forget my stuff, mate, it isn't important . . . Ralph!'

I could see Nathan now, partially hidden behind a jigsaw of steel beams and mesh panels.

I watched with fascinated terror the painfully slow journey of this kid Ralph along the roof. He was taller than us. Taller and skinnier than most kids I knew. When he moved forward his legs were like the points of a compass, spinning in mid-air. It was like watching a beginner on a surfboard; any second now and he'd tip off balance. But Ralph had only concrete to break his fall.

'Listen, Ralph,' Nathan continued, 'I don't really need that stuff. The blade on the pocket-knife is all rusty and shit, and I can always get back into the house through the shop. Ralph, get back here . . . please.'

Please?

Please?

Nathan Welsh never ever said please to anyone.

I didn't see Ralph get Nathan's things, but I did hear

Nathan whisper in a voice tight with fear, 'Don't you fall, Ralph. Please, don't you fall.'

Moving along the catwalk was one thing, but creeping along the roof of one of the silos was sheer madness. Yet barefooted and with no apparent sense of fear, Ralph managed to save my neck.

I got on my knees and peered down to the lower deck. I could see Nathan shaking his head, running a hand through his hair and crouching over Ralph.

Nathan must have seen me out of the corners of his eyes because he suddenly narrowed them in my direction and spat out angrily, 'If Ralph had fallen, Martinesi, your life wouldn't have been worth shit! Do you understand me? Shit, Martinesi. Your life wouldn't have been worth pissing on.'

I pulled my head up and swallowed too hard. While I spluttered and coughed, Nathan and Ralph climbed back onto the catwalk.

'You're a bloody menace, Martinesi,' Nathan snapped. 'A fat wog menace. How d'you reckon you'd feel right now if Ralph had gone over the edge, eh? How?'

Maybe it was the humiliation I felt, the sense of being wronged, but I stood up, and shouted right into Nathan's face. 'You're the one who scared me with that stupid sick joke! No one told him to go out there.' I pointed at Ralph where he stood silent behind Nathan. 'I didn't tell him to go risk his neck for the sake of your bloody stuff ... If he's stupid enough to go out there then bad luck if he falls.'

Before I could duck Nathan caught me on the chin with a jab to take my head off. I fell, my head snapping back and forward.

When he came at me again I knew from the look in his

eyes that he would pulp me. But before he could land a second blow Ralph had him in a head and shoulder lock.

'LET GOA'ME, RALPH,' Nathan yelled, 'LET GO.'

My jaw felt as though it had been forced all the way to the back of my skull.

'No more punching,' I heard Ralph say through my daze. That was all he said, his voice soft and non-threatening.

For a few long moments Nathan struggled, twisting and turning but unable to break Ralph's hold.

'No more punching,' Ralph repeated in the same soft voice. 'No more.'

Nathan gave a few more savage shrugs before Ralph finally set him free, one hand firm against Nathan's chest. He held Nathan out at arm's length and looked right at him. Nathan looked past him at me. Then he slowly flexed his shoulders, bit his lip and, exasperated, turned to Ralph.

Nathan took a deep breath and Ralph dropped his hand. An instant later Nathan lunged in my direction. 'GET UP!' he barked into my face. But he didn't touch me. 'Get up,' he repeated through gritted teeth.

I did, with some help from Ralph. Nothing more was said until we were back at the ladder, then Nathan, who was ahead of Ralph, turned and whispered. 'You say one word about today to anyone, Martinesi, and Ralph won't be around to save your neck, got it?'

I nodded, puzzled by the influence this Ralph seemed to have over Nathan. Nathan, who led everyone and everything at school.

'Did you hear me, Martinesi?'

I nodded.

'What?'

'Yeah, I heard.'

'I hope so, Martinesi,' Nathan seethed, 'I bloody hope so.'

Strangely, Ralph gave me the thumbs up and an enormous grin, as though we were partners.

At the foot of the ladder Nathan dismissed me abruptly, but not before he told Ralph who I was: a bookworm from school.

Not a stay-at-home, but a bookworm.

2

Mum was waiting for me as I came in the back gate.

'I doan have enough to do, do I?' she shot through pursed lips, looking up from the red peppers she was stringing together.

I didn't meet her eyes, looking instead at Rose, two years younger than me, who stood shelling peas.

'Perhaps when Rosa has finished with the peas you could convince her to do your job as well,' said Mum curtly. She turned and walked off, leaving the grill my father had welded together from leftover bits of steel on the ground at my feet. When she was almost at the laundry she paused and called back over her shoulder, 'How you Nonna is?'

'Fine,' I answered much too quickly. I swallowed hard and pointed at the tear in my shorts. 'It's just a small rip, Mum. Rose or you'll be able to sew it up no problems.'

I saw Mum stiffen. She knew. She knew I hadn't gone to my Nonna's house that morning as I'd said I would. I picked up the grill and marched off to clean it, not realising until I had filled a bucket with hot water and detergent that it had already been cleaned and was spotless.

'Davide,' my mother prompted, pronouncing my name in Italian like she did when she was being either very affectionate or very patient. 'Davide, Nonna she come, yes?'

I set the grill aside and emptied out the bucket.

'You tell to her bring the stroppoli for the ice-cream?'

'Strawberries? I . . . I think I forgot about the strawberries.'

'You forgot. What for you forgot, Davide?' My mother circled me, her arms folded. 'You remember I say to you plis ask you Nonna to bring it stroppoli for the ice-cream, yes or no?'

'I'll run back now, Ma,' I offered. 'I think I just forgot about the strawberries, and . . .'

I caught sight of Rose staring at me, her eyes wide, moving her head from side to side. We both knew I'd fallen into a web and with every word was getting more and more entangled.

I ought to have kept quiet, Rose was signalling me, especially once Mum started speaking her version of English. It had been a sign. Rose, as usual, hadn't missed it.

'Maibe you is bisi dis morning with ghelfren,' my mother went on in a huff. 'I telled you perhaps hundred times, your age ghelfren no good. Ghelfren brings you trouble.' Then in her more familiar Italian she asked, 'Davide, are you chasing girls?' And before I could answer she added, as always, 'You have to think about school, about your studies. Girls are for later . . . Now, tell me the truth, did you go meet some girl and . . . and that is how you ripped your . . . ?'

She didn't need to finish her question. I got the idea. 'No Ma, I didn't meet a girl. And yes Ma, I know I have to think about school.'

'No ghelfren?'

'No, no ghelfren, Ma. I was with some of the guys from school. I'm sorry, I got caught up with them having a kick of the footy and forgot about Nonna. I'm sorry, Ma.'

What really bothered me was that my mother need not have worried. Girls never approached me, and I . . . well the only thing missing from my allergy to girls was a visible rash on contact – eye contact.

'Rosa,' my mother called in Italian, 'come with me, we're going to your Nonna.' Then more quietly to me, 'That boy who came this morning, who was he? I haven't seen him before.'

The reason she had never seen Nathan before was that he'd never come anywhere near our house before, even though he lived in a flat over the corner milk bar, the same milk bar my father brought the bread home from every other night.

'A friend,' I answered, knowing this wasn't even a half truth. But how else could I describe Nathan: a bully, a thug, one of the divine sporting gods?

'I don't like the look of him,' my mum continued. 'He has red hair like the devil.'

'He's a good kid, Ma. He hasn't got many friends at school so, so I thought I'd, you know, get to know him.'

'You would do better to get to know your school work a little better,' Mum answered, the anger suddenly washed from her words. 'Mai son the fren to evrihuan . . . eh, Davide.' She hugged me about the head, my face pressed into her soft belly, warm and soft and safe.

'Fren to evrihuan but not the ghels yet, okay,' she laughed.

'Sure, Ma,' I called after her, 'good ol' David, friend to every man and his dog, but not the girls, Ma, never the girls.'

Oh, how I prayed to every saint my mum and Nonna had ever put faith in, that Dad and Mr Valdo would hit it off at the barbecue that afternoon. They had to, just had to. Our going to Phillip Island depended on it.

14

It might have been Mum's suggestion that we go on a holiday with the Valdos, but Dad had to feel that he was the one making the final decision.

Mr and Mrs Valdo turned up right on time. Mr Valdo brought along his tent, and suggested that Dad and I help him practise putting it up.

'Marco,' Mr Valdo explained in his quiet manner, 'last year I was very embarrassed because I couldn't even get the poles into place! I had to ask some of the campers around us to show me. I thought that maybe you and me, together we . . .'

Surprisingly, my father just laughed and with a slow wink in my direction said, 'But this year perhaps you will have the Martinesi know-how, Pietro. You didn't have that last year.' Then reverting to English he told me, 'I doan think it be too hard for the Martinesi men to put up one little tent like this. What you think, David? You think maibe me and you can put up such a small things like a tent?'

'I dunno, Dad,' I answered. We – the Martinesi men – had never even seen a tent, let alone erected one.

My father knotted his brow and leaned towards me. 'Orright,' he huffed finally, 'orright, bring the tent inna the park and we see how is we can put it up, okay?'

One of my major responsibilities with the Great Erection, as Nathan came to call it, was to number all the poles and arrange the ropes while Dad took notes and drew elaborate sketches, refusing to follow the printed instructions. 'What they tink we is, ignorante?' he'd said.

Hours later, with Mum calling us to get the barbecue started, the tent still remained nothing more than a heap of bits and pieces. Dad had misplaced the instruction booklet and couldn't find the key page of his own notes.

From the kitchen window overlooking the park Mum

watched us: she wasn't surprised by any of it.

All the while I tugged and pulled, hoisted and tied, lifted and dropped as directed. All the while I was oblivious of Nathan and Ralph, who also watched but from their perch in the silos. Then came Nathan's voice instructing from on high, 'Get the centre pole in place first, then assemble the main frame and leave the door to last!'

Dad, Mr Valdo and I looked round, but only I looked directly at the source of the advice. The lower deck of the silos on which Nathan and Ralph sat was hidden from below, and only if you knew exactly where to look and stared closely could you see anything there at all. Dad and Mr Valdo mumbled something about cheeky know-alls and returned to their heap of poles.

'Davide,' my father snapped, 'grab it the pole and hold up – there near Peter – Peter, you hold other side and . . .' But Dad got no further. The pole he was so delicately balancing above his head slipped and knocked him down with one blow.

After we'd got Dad upright again, checked him for signs of serious injury and made him sip water, Mr Valdo and I thought we'd leave the tent in the hands of the saints. They would have to look after the plight of misguided, stubborn would-be holidaymakers like us.

'Hey, Martinesi,' Nathan Welsh yelled from the silos as Mr Valdo and I helped Dad indoors, 'Next time book a caravan!'

When I glanced up Mr Valdo was frowning in my direction.

Bloody Nathan Welsh, I thought. Trust him to get me into trouble.

We did go back to the tent eventually, and by some miracle we managed to get it up. Dad and Mr Valdo were happy.

Mr Valdo took great pleasure in complimenting Dad about his food, his home, Rose and me – even my mother.

'Your wife is a very intelligent woman, Marco,' he said, within earshot of her. 'She obviously had her pick of suitors and chose one who could provide for her and her family.'

Dad, ever eager to please, and convinced that his family was a reflection of his own finer qualities, put his arm about Mr Valdo's shoulders and, encouraged by a mixture of wine and food, extolled the virtues of hard work, loyalty to one's employer and Australia.

'Five long years I wait for someone come take me from Hell,' Dad told Mr Valdo in the same mixture of anger and resentment he always used when telling his story about getting out of Italy. 'This country she is a Paradise, Pietro – you not mind me call you Pietro? This country has perfume even in the wind.' He drew a deep breath and closed his eyes.

My mother's nostrils twitched in annoyance. 'Marco, is better not bring up all that is best left to die,' she whispered. I wished she hadn't. A disagreement between my parents about leaving your native country behind was sure to prove disastrous.

'What die, die,' my father growled. 'Nothing can be more dead than what is keep the people nothing more than poor ignorant farmers. You tink the life in our village is better now than was thirty years ago – even ten years ago?' Dad cast an arm through the air and looked at me.

'Davide,' he said stiffly, 'tell you mama what sort of life you can have in her village. Tell her how much fun it be for you to herd goats and pigs all the day, and come home at night to a table what not got even enough food to feed the mice which crawl all over the floor like the moving carpet.

'But you were not born in the village, and that is good.'

Dad leaned in my mother's direction, taking in my Nonna where she sat staring at him through narrowed eyes. 'When you people talk about going back there I have to ask, why? Why? Why would anyone wish to go back to eating that what is alive with weevils and mice, feeding ten to a bowl like animals, when here, here you can have ten bowls each if you work hard enough.'

Mum often spoke of Italy and her native town with some fondness, but Dad said it was all just gibberish. According to him, after the war Italy had become nothing but a battle-ravaged ruin. The war, the Fascists, the Germans, and even the Allies who liberated her had raped Italy and made her barren. Robbed of skills, starved of education, forced to watch the North thrive under mismanaged post-war economic restructure while his beloved Mezzogiorno fell ever more backward into the feudal agricultural ways of old, my father hadn't been able to get out quickly enough.

But Mum said that given the correct circumstances life in one's native land was always infinitely better than life in a country like Australia where the language itself was the least foreign part of the new equation. Dad, on the other hand, said that if it wasn't for Australia and its promise to migrants, my mother would still be herding goats and dressing in hand-me-downs.

'Marco,' my mother said in a voice borrowed from whatever saint it was who oversaw patience, 'Pietro and la signora is not here to listen you talk bout dis things.'

'No, you is right,' my father snapped. 'Only Dellavecchia really can unnerstand what means to me to be free of that misery.'

Signor Giuseppe Dellavecchia was a short but very lean man, fifteen years older than Dad, with thinning grey hair, a thick moustache and eyes the size of large broad beans.

He had sponsored my father's immigration to Australia. He was always impeccably dressed: a dark blue or grey suit, shirt, tie and always, always the same flannel waistcoat with the three brass buttons I had found so fascinating as a little kid. He had settled in Australia just after World War II, and was supposedly a very successful tobacco farmer, with properties all over Victoria and southern New South Wales. The word was that Signor Dellavecchia, a native of my father's home village, made his real money from exploiting the fit young men he had sponsored out of 'Hell'.

'That man could dance with the devil himself and not be burnt,' said Nonna. She disliked Dellavecchia even more than Mum did.

That was it, I told myself. That was the end of all decent conversation for the night. My Nonna and her son-in-law never saw much to agree upon anyway, but introduce Giuseppe Dellavecchia into the discussion and there was no room for compromise.

Rose came and stood beside me and rolled her eyes. 'Maybe Mr Valdo will feel sorry for us and take us all to Phillip Island anyway,' she whispered.

No one spoke for a few minutes. My father stood shaking his head and pouring out more of his special grappa, most of it onto his shoes. Mr Valdo stuffed his mouth with more of Nonna's taralli biscuits in an effort, I guess, to keep from being drawn into taking sides, while his wife smiled distractedly from behind a cup of tea Rose had made for her.

'Here, Dad,' I said, taking the bottle from him, 'let me fill your glass.' And as I did he kissed the top of my head and ruffled my hair.

'You is a good boy, Davide,' he said rather formally. 'Your *compare* and me have great expectations for you. You will be someone, for certain. You will be something for to be much proud.'

'Sure, Dad,' I reassured him, as I did every time Dellavecchia came round unexpectedly.

'No worries for sure,' my father reiterated. 'This not Italy. This not some *village.*'

That was it, then. I realised that Dad had finally reached his decision. The Martinesi family were going on holiday!

I turned to smile at Rose and saw a movement down amongst the shadows by the back fence. It only took me a moment to realise who it was. The footy beanie gave him away.

I sidled towards him. 'Ralph!' I whispered, 'get outta here will you! If my old man or my mum see you, you're in big shit.' Actually, I'd be the one in the shit.

Ralph, smiling, peeped over the oil drum again, footy beanie pulled low over his ears. 'Smells good,' he said. He was looking past me to where the others were feasting.

'Listen Ralph, thanks for saving my neck with Nathan this morning, but this really isn't a good time to come pay a visit, okay.' I turned to go, hoping he would take the hint.

'Smells good,' Ralph repeated, only now he was looking at the food in my hands, a sausage smothered in sauce with a dash of lemon.

'You want this?' I asked, holding my food out to him. I glanced quickly over my shoulder, hoping that no one had noticed us. 'If I give you my food, will you go away, please?'

Ralph didn't reply. He was already holding a hand out for my bribe.

'Don't they feed you at the dog's home?' I quipped, and the moment I had, I was sorry. Ralph stopped chewing, his face distorted by the bulges in his cheeks, and blinked back at me.

'It was a joke,' I tried. 'Shit, Ralph, don't you know a joke from an insult? I would've thought being around Nathan Welsh would've taught you the difference.'

I glanced back toward Mum, who was now serving up dessert and coffee. Any minute now she would be asking after me, the son who never missed sweets.

'Where's Nathan, still up on the silos?' I asked. I looked past Ralph. I wanted to say something clever, something that would let Nathan Welsh know that I was up with his antics, and didn't he know that this was my house and I could get my dad onto him just like that!

I looked quickly back at Ralph and swallowed hard. 'I bet it's a real scream for you and Nathan to go around doing this sort of shit,' I said. 'I bet Nathan Welsh gets a real kick out of agitating poor old stay-at-home dicks like David Martinesi. That was real funny you know, that shit about the tent this afternoon. Listen, why don't you just go back to Nathan and leave me alone, okay. Go on.'

'Nathan gone to church,' Ralph said simply. He was chewing again but something had gone out behind his eyes and he looked at me blankly.

'Yeah, and the Pope's dropping in to my place in a few minutes for an audience with my Nonna,' I snapped back, angrier now as it occurred to me just how much was at stake if either of my parents spotted Ralph.

Ralph shook his head. 'Today's Saturday. Nathan gone church.'

There was a heaviness in Ralph's voice that slapped into me. He didn't seem retarded exactly, just ... simple. Very simple. Like a really young kid. I couldn't remember ever having seen Ralph before that morning, which was strange given the way he and Nathan seemed to know each other. But then Ralph wasn't exactly the sort of kid you'd look at

21

twice. Still, it didn't make sense. Nathan Welsh wasn't short of hangers-on, so why did he seem so interested in this kid? Ralph was just like the kids Nathan loved to get stuck into at school. He was more like me than he was like Nathan.

'You gotta go, Ralph, the Pope's just arrived,' I said more harshly than necessary. Then to my mother, who stood with coffee pot in mid-pour, I called, 'Just a sec, Ma.'

When I turned back to tell Ralph that Nathan was pretty stupid for daring him to come into our back yard like this, Ralph had gone. 'Ralph?' I whispered. 'Ralph, you there?'

I felt empty and unsettled, not so much because Ralph had come into my private world, but because somehow I believed him about Nathan Welsh being at church.

3

Nathan was hanging off our back fence next morning when I went out to feed the hen Mum had bought from a poultry-farmer the day before. I didn't see Nathan until I'd already made an idiot of myself clucking at the hen as she squawked from her temporary home under an upturned crate.

'You bloody wogs'll eat anything,' he said.

I spilt some of the seed I'd been scooping through the slats of the crate.

'Next thing you know, you'll be hanging pig carcasses off your fig tree.'

I stopped what I was doing and stood up, bowl in hand.

'Christ, Martinesi, you're a sorry sight,' Nathan sniggered, and with a single push he was up and onto the fence. He sat there, his legs dangling just short of my face. I tried hard to ignore him.

'You don't have to keep chooks in the back yard any more you know,' he said through a half grin. 'Haven't you people ever heard of KFC?'

'I've gotta finish this,' I said. Even doing something as

normal as feeding the chook had suddenly pitted Nathan against me. I turned to go, hoping Nathan would too.

'This is a special hen,' I lied. 'Of course ah . . . Dad usually runs down . . . drives really, Dad drives down to KFC.'

Shit, I thought, watching him. Shit, now the entire school would get to know about the hen and me feeding it. I could almost hear the new nickname: Martinesi the Chicken Handler. Nathan jumped down and walked around me, his eyes on the crate at my feet, scratching his head.

'It belongs to my Nonna – my grandmother. She asked us to look after it for her.'

Minutes passed without a comment from either of us, just the sound of the hen cackling away under the crate. Then Nathan asked, 'You got time to come down to the creek this afternoon?'

I stopped. Had I heard right? He couldn't be asking me to join him. I tensed, half expecting a dare to be issued.

'You ever get to, you know . . .' Nathan changed direction suddenly and snapped an imaginary hen's neck mid-air. I shook my head. 'Nah, didn't think so . . . Poor thing, what a way to go.'

'They don't suffer,' I cut in. 'Dad's real quick.'

Nathan chuckled. 'So's the electric chair.'

'Ralph gate-crashed our barbecue,' I said.

'I wouldn't worry too much about it. Ralph's like that sometimes.'

'Like what?'

Nathan ignored me. 'What did Ralph have to say . . . when he gate-crashed your barbecue?'

I shrugged my shoulders, unsure whether to mention the bit about church. I decided not to. 'I gave him a sausage,' I said.

There was a moment when it seemed Nathan might tell

me something. He scratched the nape of his neck, drew lightly on his smoke, then flicked the butt away without a word.

'Now what're you doing, Martinesi?' he asked when I pounced on the still smouldering stump of his cigarette.

'If my old man sees this I'm gone!'

Nathan rolled his eyes and poked his tongue hard into his cheek.

I tossed the butt over the fence and told Nathan I had to go. But Nathan was having a closer look at the hen and wasn't in any hurry to leave.

'You gotta go, Nathan,' I stammered uneasily.

'You don't eat dogs' balls as well, d'you?' Nathan said, and before I could react he had the crate off the ground and the crazed hen dangling by its feet.

'Nathan ... please. Please put the hen back, please.' I didn't want to plead, but I didn't want anything to happen to Mum's hen either. The hen flapped her tattered wings fiercely, but Nathan held her firmly and danced her round and round in ever faster circles.

'Pl-ea-se Nathan, drop the hen!' I wailed.

And Nathan did. He just let the hen drop, and she went scurrying all over Dad's vegie patch trying to escape.

'BASTARD!' I yelled into Nathan's face. I ducked and dived and fell over myself trying to catch the hen. The commotion brought Rose out and she stood by the back door watching me with silent, accusing eyes.

I pulled myself to my full height and yelled at her to go back inside and stop staring. But Rose didn't. She merely folded her arms and shook her head in my direction.

When I finally looked round, the hen was safely preening herself on the garage roof and Nathan was nowhere in sight.

I realised then that I couldn't afford not to go to the creek that afternoon.

'I got into heaps of trouble with my mum over that chicken,' I told Nathan the moment I saw him. He was sitting on the grass under the Merri Merri bridge, his knees up close to his chest. He didn't even bother to look round.

'Took your time coming,' he said finally. 'When I said this afternoon, I kinda meant two or three o'clock, not four-thirty.'

'If you hadn't let the hen out I wouldn't have had to spend the afternoon clearing out our garage.'

'Why didn't you just tell her it was me who did it?' Nathan replied calmly, daring me to answer. Then he went back to looking at the slimy shallow water of the creek. I put my hands in my pockets and stood looking up and down the creek bank. There was no one else around, and only a few cars on the bridge. Behind us the primary school was locked deep in its holiday silence.

This was all too odd. Here I was with Nathan Welsh and we had nothing at all in common. What was I doing here?

'What d'you want?' I asked and swallowed hard. Obviously Nathan had been checking me out, otherwise he couldn't have known about my spot here at the creek.

'If you're going to have a go at me then just get it over with,' I challenged. 'I didn't mean to embarrass you at school over the Phillip Island thing. And I took your punch ... I even climbed the frigging silos 'cos you made me ... And that stuff about me being responsible for your mate Ralph risking his life on the silo is just bullshit! There's no way I made him go out on that roof ... no way ...'

Ralph's sudden appearance at the barbecue, the advice about the tent, and Nathan jumping the back fence – all of it was just Nathan's way of stirring me. It had to be a payback for Ralph almost making a martyr of himself on top of the silos.

There was a splash out in the middle of the creek and I jumped. Nathan had tossed a stone and ripples spread in perfect circles on the water's surface.

'You're not going to Phillip Island, Welsh.' I decided now that I really had nothing to lose. 'You just said that to get on my back.' I took a few steps forward, down the embankment. 'At first I thought you were going, but now I reckon it's just more of your bullshit, your way of staying on my back so that all your so-called mates will think you're such a hero.'

Nathan didn't utter a word. He shook his head, brushed the grass from his jeans and took to the bike path on foot.

'You shoot pool, Martinesi?' he called over his shoulder when he was almost out of sight.

And that's when I saw Ralph. He was seated in the fork of a willow, dangling a hand line in the creek. He waved when he saw me but I was too preoccupied to respond. The moment Nathan was at the foot of the tree Ralph frantically gathered up his line and jumped from his perch.

'Come on,' he said through a smile. Then he followed Nathan at a short distance.

St George's Road had never been a bustling shopping strip, but today only George's Fish 'n' Chip Shop, Concetta's Laundromat and Fernando's Café were open.

I'd never been inside Fernando's. It had never actually been said out loud that I was not to go into Fernando's but I knew that if I was ever caught inside, or word got back to my parents that I had, not even the grace of God would save me. The men in that place were liars, small-time crooks, professionally unemployed, or plain losers. I'd heard Dad tell Rose that once when she'd asked why he never took us there to buy a gelati.

Fernando's was gloomy even from the outside. A hand-written sign on the window asked patrons to leave their coats on the hooks provided, and other people's business where they heard it. Fernando's caricature – a portly man with a rogue moustache and dark eyes – was barely recognisable on either of the once-colourful awnings that hung limp and faded, their frayed tassels draped over the door and veranda.

'Feeble-minded men take their chances in that place,' Dad had often told me. 'They gamble and lose a week's wages. They take food from the mouths of their children.'

I took a deep breath and rushed head first through the doorway, past the old pinball machines that lined one wall, past the heavy-set and bespectacled man behind the coffee machine, to where Nathan was already setting the balls up on a pool table at the back of the café.

'Ralph, winner plays Martinesi, okay,' Nathan announced, and I wished for once he'd called me David.

Someone yelled abuse and I looked round. A man at one of the window tables was yelling at another man, his hands cutting the air wildly. Busy with their game, neither Nathan nor Ralph appeared to notice. My mouth dried and I swallowed air too quickly. I wished I'd never come. Dad had been right. Even if I was fifteen, in this place I was still just a kid. This was not a place for good and decent men.

'You're up.' Nathan pushed me back on my heels roughly. 'Watch out for Ralph though, the man shoots mean pool.'

The cue slipped in my hands.

'Your turn, Martinesi.' Nathan must have noticed the

unease on my face because he patted me lightly on the cheek and edged me towards the table. 'Your break,' he said flatly. Ralph grinned at him.

I stood motionless at the head of the table, staring down at the balls at the opposite end. 'I really shouldn't be here,' I stammered and would have handed the cue back to Nathan if he hadn't moved towards the bar. At the other end of the table Ralph nodded his head at me and motioned that I should break.

'You going to break or what, Martinesi?' The impatient edge was back in Nathan's voice. He was tearing the cellophane from a packet of cigarettes he'd just bought.

'It's late,' I replied.

'And it'll be even later before you break. Now just PLAY!'

I didn't want to play pool. I didn't want to do anything except leave. I glanced at Ralph for support but he just wanted me to hit the white ball.

At the bar the bespectacled man was leaning across the counter watching us in a disinterested sort of way and yawned.

'You've got more hang-ups than a picture shop, Martinesi,' Nathan jeered. 'Just hit the fucking white ball.'

'Boy,' the barman bawled out, 'what is problem?'

Nathan spun on his heels. 'Nothing, just talking about the game, that's all.'

The barman cocked his head and stared down his nose at us, at me. 'You want play, play,' he advised. 'If not, go home, hokay?'

Nathan nudged me. 'We're playing.'

My break was a total farce, the white ball shooting off the end of the table and bouncing into the door behind Ralph.

'Yeah, right, good shot, Martinesi,' Nathan laughed. 'Another shot like that and you'll bring the boys from the back room out. And the boys in the back room play serious cards and shit, and don't wanna be disturbed ...'

Just then the back door opened and a short man in a tight shirt and baggy shorts poked his head out. 'Fernando, *tre espresso e un caffelatte,*' he called to the barman. Then he was gone, the door shut behind him.

'Don't look so surprised,' Nathan laughed into my ear. 'The *real* gamblers need peace and quiet.' He nodded toward the window tables. 'Those guys just play for tens and twenties. In there ...' He lowered his voice. 'In there they play for life savings. Come here often enough and you see people going in and out. You hear a word here or there ...'

'But you're not even Italian,' I observed.

'Really?' Nathan said in mock horror. 'That'll be news to my mum. Half the blokes who come here aren't Italian, Martinesi, so get real.'

We watched in silence as the barman carefully balanced a tray with the coffees on it and plodded to the door. He knocked three times. When the door opened, he handed the tray in without entering. Then he waved a hand in our direction saying, 'You play or you go?'

Ralph was way too good a player for me. He pocketed balls easily, even the most difficult shots.

'He thinks he's the next Australian billiard champ,' Nathan mocked, though without his usual venom. 'Isn't that right, Ralph?'

'Nah,' smirked Ralph. 'Not Australia. The world.'

'Yeah, right, Ralph,' Nathan replied, 'and I'm the next principal of St Joe's.'

They laughed then, the two of them. But still Ralph wasn't exactly what I thought of as being Nathan's type of mate. Ralph didn't seem to be altogether there. There was something in the too gross movements of his arms and legs – as if they were all too large – and in the stoop of his shoulders, as though a weight sat right on his neck. And it was there in his smile, a little too ready, too casual. Simple. It was the only label I could think of.

What was even stranger though was the fact that Nathan had never once, in all the years we'd been in the same class, mentioned Ralph, even in passing. Either their friendship was new or Ralph was a major secret. And if a secret, why? And why had I been introduced to him?

'You reckon you could concentrate on the game long enough to know whose shot it is?'

'Wha – oh, sorry.' I aimed and potted the black. I'd lost.

Nathan slammed his cue on the table. 'Shit, Martinesi, what d'you do for fun – lick stamps!'

'Ei ... Ei ... you boys break sticks, you pay for new ones, you unnerstand me,' the barman bellowed. He wiped his hands on a dish towel that hung over his shoulder and narrowed his eyes.

'Relax mister ... nothing's broken ... hokay.' Nathan turned and winked at Ralph, who grinned right back at him and then at me.

Just then the back door opened again and from behind a thin veil of light and smoke someone called, 'Fernando! Fernando! *Porti la birra.* Fernando! Beer, Fernando!' A moment later the door was pushed wide open.

That was when I saw him. That was when I saw what I never ever imagined I'd see, and for a long time wished I hadn't seen.

My dad.

There he was, standing beside the man who'd ordered the coffees. He stood with one arm slung amicably over this man's shoulder.

I stood and stared at my father.

He never once looked round into the café all the time the door was open. I stood rooted to the spot like some blinded rabbit caught in the glare of the shooter's lamp.

Only Dellavecchia glanced up for a moment from his seat at a table where two other men sat looking sullen and distracted. If he recognised me, nothing on his face showed it. He went right on laughing into the space between us as though no one but him was there.

4

For days after spotting my dad at Fernando's I didn't see either Nathan Welsh or Ralph much. But that didn't worry me. What did was that I couldn't look at my father for more than a few moments without being overwhelmed by a sense of betrayal. He'd let me down. I couldn't say anything to him. What could I say, after all? Hey, you've been lying to me all this time about Fernando's! How could I explain that I'd seen him in Fernando's in the first place? And even if I did tell him, then what?

So I decided that for the time being I'd forget about it and join in the Christmas celebrations instead.

Dad had probably just been in Fernando's because he'd been forced to keep Dellavecchia company again, that was all.

Still, the long drive to Zio Frank's place for Christmas Eve dinner was a bit touch and go for a while, especially when I said that I couldn't see the point of Compare Dellavecchia's constant and uninvited visits.

'You'd think he had nowhere else to go, no one else to bug,' I said with just enough of a laugh to take the sarcasm out of my tone.

Beside me Nonna made a kind of gurgling noise, like a fart, but from her mouth.

At the very next set of traffic lights my father spun round and hit me with the back of his hand.

'What did you do that for?' I yelped.

'Because you have to learn respect.' My father's voice was brittle with annoyance and his fingers gripped the steering wheel.

'Yeah,' cut in Rose, 'it's not as though he visits and doesn't bring you anything.'

'Great, Rose,' I snapped back. 'He brings me really good stuff that I can use the next time I'm seven or eight years old.'

'Stop it, both of you,' our mother demanded in her best Italian. And turning on our father, she spat, 'That man overstays his welcome every time he comes, Marco, that's all. I'd like to know a little ahead of time that he might be dropping in . . .'

'Good idea, Teresa, then the rest of us could eat somewhere else.' It was Nonna, putting in her ten cents worth.

Dad slowed the car down so he could look back at Rose, Nonna and me crumpled against one another in the back. 'If you don't like the company I choose to bring to *my* house then perhaps you could stay in your *own* house and eat there on a Sunday.'

Nonna made another of her farting sounds and straightened her back. She looked first at Mum, then at Rose and finally at me. 'You poor creatures,' she whispered, 'that crude man's ways have rubbed off on your father.'

The car screeched to a halt. Dad turned and faced the rest of us, his face flushed crimson and his eyes darting. 'Anyone who is not content with the way this family is run can open the door right this minute and leave.'

That about saw the Christmas spirit fly out the window. From that moment until we arrived at Zio Frank's, and for some time after, Mum argued with Dad, Dad argued with Mum, Nonna argued with whoever of my parents wasn't arguing with the other, and occasionally both Mum and Dad argued with Nonna.

Zio Frank and Zia Gina were waiting for us when we arrived and, as usual, they bear-hugged each of us in turn. When Zio got to Rose he held her out at arm's length as though he hadn't seen her in years.

'Too beautiful,' he sighed with feigned surprise. Then to Rose herself, 'One day you will make a very good wife and mother.'

'Rosa is only a baby yet, Franco,' Zia Gina cut in. 'Come, let me show you what I've bought you.'

'For her glory box,' I piped up, knowing how much Rose hated our aunt constantly buying sheets, pillow cases, crocheted bedspreads, and pots and pans for her 'to have when the time is right'. The 'time', of course, being the day some poor unfortunate married her, as I liked to remind Rose.

My mother's look was cold to the bone. 'A girl can never have enough,' she hissed in my direction. 'Gina, you're too kind.' And she was, especially as she had no children of her own to dote upon.

Zia Gina wouldn't have noticed the joke at her expense. Like her husband, she was one of those people who never did anyone any harm, never put a foot wrong, never lost their cool. They were . . . well, they were boring. Lovable, but dead boring. They had this thing about having to keep furniture new and they never allowed anyone but the most particular guests to sit in their lounge room. So I waltzed right through the house, past the kitchen where the chairs had been arranged around an oversized table, and into that very room.

'Davide,' my Zio Frank called me back. 'We're in here.'

'Sorry, Zio,' I grinned. 'Guess I just lost my mind there for a moment.'

My uncle's eyes followed me as I walked back to the kitchen and sidled up to the table, and helped myself to a rice ball.

'The furniture,' my uncle began explaining, but shrugged his shoulders instead.

'I understand, Zio,' I replied, my mouth full. 'Imagine actually having a human bum on one of those chairs . . .'

My father was at the window staring out into the garden. He looked round at me and narrowed his eyes. 'Some people work hard for what they have. They can do with it what they want.'

Rose shuffled back into the kitchen, her face long and her eyes hooded.

I couldn't resist it. 'What did you get this time, a frypan? An eggtimer? No, wait . . . a microwave and dishwasher combination complete with add-on toaster, lasagna dish and non-stick biscuit maker with its own cutter?'

'You're a dickhead, David, you really are,' Rose hissed, and might have said more if Nonna hadn't walked in and announced how pleased she was that at least some-one was considering her grand-daughter's needs for the future.

'What if she decides not to get married?' I asked Nonna around a second arrancino.

Nonna made one of her farting sounds again and put an arm around Rose. 'With these hips what else can she do, become a pilot?' She squeezed Rose tightly to her, planting a wet kiss on her forehead. Rose rolled her eyes and swallowed back her reply so she wouldn't chill the old lady into an early grave.

'What did you get, Rose?' I asked more quietly as I helped her out from under Nonna's arm.

'An electric blanket,' Rose replied, the corner of her mouth sharp with reproach.

'Well, that'll be great for Mr Rose Martinesi, Sis. At least he can thaw out on that, hey.'

Rose didn't want to grin, but finally she did. 'You'd better believe it, Mister,' she said.

'You're lucky Mum didn't see your friends in the back yard this afternoon,' Rose said when the two of us had managed to escape outdoors after the meal. She looked at me with searching eyes. 'Yes, I did see them. Two of them. You were talking to them over the fence when you were supposed to have been watering Dad's tomatoes.'

Rose rolled her eyes and exhaled loudly. 'I see a lot more than you think, Big Brother,' she sneered. 'You were there talking to them for ages.'

'So?'

'One of those boys was Nathan Welsh from down the shop. I recognised him straight off. He looks like a beetroot with that red hair ...' Rose looked back over her shoulder. 'He's not exactly the sort of kid Mum or Dad would ever want in our house you know ... I bet he was the one who let the hen run loose too.'

'Sometimes you talk shit, Rose.'

'Maybe. Maybe not. But I did see you standing by the back fence talking to Nathan Welsh and some other guy.'

Like Mum, Rose was just like a shadow sometimes; there, yet not there, unless you took the trouble to look for her, or you stumbled upon her. We never actually talked much, not in any deep sense, yet I knew Rose was pretty much like our mother – someone to be reckoned with. Nathan Welsh would've said that Rose had balls.

'Did you tell Mum the truth about the hen?' I asked quietly.

'That Nathan Welsh let it loose? No.'

I nodded and tried to focus on the music.

Silver bells. Silver bells. Soon it will be Christmas D-ay . . .

'Who was that guy with Nathan?'

'Just a mate of his.'

'No name?'

'What do you reckon?'

Rose raised her eyebrows in the same way Nonna did when she thought you were being stupid.

'Ralph.'

'Ralph?' Rose laughed. 'Ralph what?'

'Does it matter?' My voice rose in annoyance.

'Nope, I guess not,' Rose looked back toward the others. Nonna was consulting her watch. 'Must be almost time for us to go to Mass. She must think everyone in Melbourne goes to St Leo's for midnight Mass the way she goes on about having to get there early.'

'She wants a seat, Rose. She's old, she can't handle having to stand.'

'She can have mine.'

'Yeah, right Rose, and you'll be the martyr and stand in the aisles.'

'I'd rather not go.'

This caught me by surprise, for besides having Christmas Eve dinner at Zio Frank's, another sacred Martinesi rite was midnight Mass at Zia Gina's church. Zio Frank himself was a card-carrying Catholic only, attendances restricted to baptisms, weddings, communions, confirmations and funerals, and only if he absolutely couldn't avoid them. He'd go, might even stay around outside and chat to the other religious zealots, but more often than not he and Dad would go back to Zio's place until it was time to 'collect the women'.

Unfortunately, Dad thought that a bit of the Holy Spirit probably wouldn't do me any harm, even if for him religion was pretty much a waste of time. He was more concerned about living than what'd happen to him after death. Leave the dead to the dead, he liked to say. Leave the dead to the dead, and the living in peace.

'You'll give Dad a heart attack if you don't go to Mass, Rose,' I said.

Rose snorted. 'He, Mum, Nonna and the whole lot of them.'

'Imagine that, hey. An entire family destroyed because a daughter fails to observe the faith.' I wanted to laugh but didn't for fear that Rose might crack up again. I needn't have worried. Rose was not about to crack up. Far from it.

'It's too easy for you, David,' Rose began slowly. 'When you're old enough Dad'll just expect you to stop going to Mass. You won't even have to come along to these sorts of nights then either, if you don't want to. Dad'll just shrug his shoulders and accept that his little boy has grown up and is doing what all Italian boys do when they get old enough.'

'Yeah, right Rose. I'll just walk up to Dad one day and tell him, "Papa, guess what? I don't want to study any more. Think I'll take off around Europe for a few years. How's about some cash . . ." '

I stopped short. This was my sister I was talking to. My almost fourteen-year-old sister.

'Phillip Island should be great,' I said, changing the subject.

'Yeah, for you maybe,' Rose replied. 'I'll probably have to cook and wash plates, air the sleeping bags, sweep the floor, tidy the tent, and maybe – just maybe, get to sit around and do nothing like you will. Except it'll be the middle of the night by then and everyone else'll be asleep.'

'It's a *holiday*, Rose. We're going on a holiday. Think about it. Us – the Martinesi's of Fitzroy going on a ho-li-day . . .'

But Rose wouldn't budge. 'You don't seem the type Nathan Welsh would hang around with. What did you do, bribe him?'

I liked Rose. I really did. But sometimes she had a way of getting up my nose.

'Of course you know a whole lot about Nathan Welsh,' I smirked as casually as I could and sat back to stare at the clear night sky.

She was silent for a while, her arms locked about her knees. Then she rested her chin on her hands and leaned towards me. 'I know a whole lot more about you, David Angelo Martinesi. I know that unlike Nathan Welsh you're a conshi student. I know that unlike Nathan Welsh you've never been in any trouble. And I know that sometimes you're too good for your own good.'

'Meaning what exactly, Madame Freud?'

Rose stared directly ahead. 'Meaning, that unlike Nathan Welsh you've got a lot to lose, Big Brother. I mean, you've never had a close friend, ever. You've never even had a mate over during the school holidays that I can remember. In fact you've never even had a birthday party where the guests weren't hand-picked by Mum and Dad, and then they were just rellos. Now suddenly you're hanging out with Nathan Welsh. It's odd, that's all.'

'Well, you seem to be friends with any bloody stray thing that needs a pat on the back or a shoulder to cry on,' I snapped. 'Shit, Rose, you've got more "friends" than Nonna has saints, and that's saying something. Don't try and tell me they're all your true and trusted mates.'

Rose laughed under her breath and the hair on my arms tingled with indignation.

'What's so funny, Miss Socialite?'

'Nothing, David Angelo Martinesi,' Rose replied. 'Nothing's funny at all.'

'You're just in the shits because Dad gave you a back-hander for answering him back at the table in front of everyone,' I told her more forcefully than I'd intended. 'It was your own fault. If you hadn't opened your big mouth then you wouldn't have been embarrassed the way you were . . .'

'Dickhead,' Rose yelled.

'Bitch,' I shot back. 'Cow . . .'

Back home the next day before lunch, we exchanged Christmas presents with the usual thanks and 'you shouldn't haves'. Only Nonna was honest enough to admit that yet another blue cardigan from Zio Paul was perhaps one too many. Zio Paul, a thirty-something bachelor, didn't take offence.

'Well, Mama,' he said without the least bit of affectation, 'at least I'm consistent.'

'Of course you are,' Zio Sandro said. 'Consistently late for family gatherings. Consistently inconsiderate of anyone else's feelings but your own.'

'That's what comes of having no sense of responsibility,' Zia Graziella said in support of her husband. 'Just wait until you find yourself a wife, have children like I do, take on the burden of a home . . . Things will have to change.'

I looked at Zio Paul. I hated it when the others ganged up on him. Of all my uncles he was my favourite. He knew how to make people relax. He was funny and didn't care if he played the fool, so long as no one got hurt. He wasn't such a tight-arse as Zio Sandro and he could loosen up and joke with us.

When he caught me looking at him, Zio Paul grinned sheepishly and winked. 'So, Dottore,' he said using the nickname he had for me, 'when you're all grown-up and have been to university, maybe you can study my brother there and find a cure for his lack of humour ...'

Zio Sandro – or Machiavelli as Zio Paul called him – scoffed at me. 'Tell the idiot to stop worrying about other people and get himself a decent job and a good woman.'

'All the decent jobs are taken, and as for good women, well, I guess the Lord stopped making them after your great find.'

Zio Sandro was lost for a comeback.

Nonna stepped in and insisted her sons stop acting like children and remember that it was Christmas Day. 'Come here the two of you and let me see you shake hands. Paolo can't help being the clown, and Sandro thinks the world has to run to a timetable like the railways.'

'Not the Italian railways,' I piped up. Rose covered her face with one hand and stared down at her plate. Zio Frank and Zia Gina sat observing, but wouldn't be drawn in.

Dad stared hard at me and I knew that he was not impressed. Mum kept right away, engrossed in getting the pasta served.

'Machia – ' Zio Paul began, then caught himself, a sly grin spreading over his face. 'Sandro, I tell you what, the day I find a good woman and get a decent job I'll be sure to settle down and follow your example.'

Zio Paul reached over and brushed a hand gently across Rose's forehead. 'So, Fiore, how's school with you? Still planning to change the world and win greater equality for the poor downtrodden women? I remember there was a

girl who went to school with me who went on to become
a journalist. The only one in the entire class to actually
make something of herself ...' He had been the only one
of Nonna's three children to start primary school in
Australia but, unlike Machiavelli, who went through to
complete the equivalent of Year 10, Zio Paul left as soon
as he could.

'What for a journalist?' Dad asked stiffly. He looked at
Rose, and I saw her take a quick breath. 'My Rose she be
the Prime Minister of Australia ...' If it was meant as a joke
neither Rose nor Zio Paul laughed. Neither did Dad.

We were well into Nonna's speciality second course, my
cousin Tony still to utter a word as usual, when Dad informed
the rest of the family about our forthcoming holiday.

'I have decided to take my family to Phillip Island for a
few days between now and the New Year,' Dad said without
missing a mouthful.

My mother was smiling thinly into her plate. He had
decided! Sure! I could just see the thought crossing her
mind. She lifted her eyes a moment and winked at me as if
to say, 'Let him believe what he likes, we're going, aren't
we?' And then she went back to her veal.

'They have a place there they call Cowes,' he went on
when no one seemed to have heard him. 'Once before a
man dies he should see such a place. Teresa's friend invited
us and I think to myself, If the chance is there why not take
it? So I take it, and we're going.'

'In a tent,' Rose added.

'And you wait until now to tell the rest of us?' Machiavelli
asked stiffly. 'You might as well have sent a postcard.' He
put down his knife and fork noisily and huffed.

For a few long moments no one spoke. Not even Dad,
who went right on with his meal as though oblivious to

Machiavelli's annoyance. Machiavelli and Zia Graziella loved to be informed about everyone else's affairs.

'Teresa, is this true?' said Zia Graziella. 'You are really going to take these poor children out in a *tent*, to a place you've never been before?'

'A tent. This is a luxury,' Nonna cut in. 'When I was a girl a tent would have seemed like a suite at the best hotel. How many nights while herding the goats did I have to sleep out in the cold under the low sky! ... How many! ... A tent ... A tent would have been paradise ...'

Zio Paul reached across and gave Dad a pat on the shoulder. 'Good on you, Marco,' he said through a huge grin. 'It's about bloody time this family starting looking beyond its own front door ... I reckon we should *all* pack it in and head down to Cowes. Who knows, maybe next year, when things are different, we can all have Christmas lunch in a tent down at Phillip Island.'

'Of course *you* can say that, can't you,' Machiavelli snapped. 'Unlike the rest of us, my brother has absolutely no sense of tradition. Let me ask you this, brother of mine; how do you think my family would feel if I were to suddenly take them into a tent, of all things, and make them miss out on the Christmas they have always known?'

'Relieved probably,' Zio Paul laughed.

'This Nathan kid, do you reckon he's levelling with you, Dottore?' Zio Paul asked when I'd finished telling him about Nathan and the Saturday morning I'd been made to climb the silos.

'How do you mean?'

Zio Paul had been around, so what he might have to say about Nathan Welsh mattered to me, and I'd told him as much. We were in the back yard, sitting on old tree stumps painted a ghastly blue. Zio Paul nursed a tumbler of scotch and seemed taken by the view – row upon row of carefully tended cucumber plants, bean shoots, sprawling eggplants, and lettuce heads along the length of the garden bed.

'He hasn't asked for anything, if that's what you mean,' I answered. 'He doesn't need to go to all this trouble just to get me to do things for him.' I stopped abruptly, aware suddenly of how pathetic I sounded. 'I mean, it's not as though I'm a lap dog or something.'

'But this Nathan kid is pretty popular, right?' my uncle cut in, still without looking at me. 'I bet he's popular and tough, and a bit of a lady killer, right?'

I nodded.

'How do you feel about his hanging around, or rather, his having you hanging around?' The question caught me by surprise and I wasn't sure how to answer. I mean, deep down, I was rapt that Nathan Welsh had asked me to go shoot pool with him. But how did I feel about the whole thing? Confused.

'You think maybe Nathan is out to do something to me?' I asked, deflated by the possibility. 'He's the kind who would, you know! He could smile right into your face and still be twisting the knife into your back.'

'You don't really believe that though, do you?' Zio Paul sat back against the wall and winked at me as he pressed his drink to my lips for a quick sip. When I coughed he smiled. 'You know what I reckon, Dottore? I reckon Nathan Welsh knows a good bloke when he sees one. I reckon Nathan and that other mate of his . . .'

'Ralph.'

'Ralph,' my uncle repeated. 'I reckon they're sick and tired of hanging around with losers and no-hopers. Believe me, I know. I've been there.' He took a deep breath. 'You see, Dottore, people like Nathan Welsh get off on being the school clown, the class hero and so on. But every now and then even a clown needs to take off the grease paint, you follow?'

I blinked and Zio Paul narrowed his eyes before going on, his voice a little lower than before. 'Maybe Nathan just needs a real friend, someone who hasn't got off on all the bullshit and put-on, someone who has a bit of decency and integrity.' Then as though to break the sombreness of his tone he added, 'How do you like that word, eh, in-te-gri-ty. I tell you what, Dottore, with just a little more commitment, and a few more mates like you, I reckon I could've finished school and gone on to be a whole lot more than a factory hand . . .'

That, I guess, was the moment when I first realised that behind my uncle's self-mocking good nature and apparent lack of care for everything that was so important to people like Machiavelli, there lay something sharp and painful, something that cut deep.

We were silent for a few minutes and I thought about what Zio Paul had said. Maybe Nathan *was* tired of the bully-boy bullshit at school. I still didn't know enough about Nathan and his motives. And I was soon to find out that I knew even less about my Zio Paul than I imagined I did.

'Dottore, can you keep a secret?' my uncle asked, turning to face me.

'Yeah,' I replied quickly, keen to dissolve the awkwardness that had settled upon us. 'You know me, the trustworthy Dottore.' I grinned through my teeth and sat forward into his shadow.

'That was a stupid question,' my uncle said softly. 'Of course I can trust my Dottore.' When he brushed me on the

46

head lightly I could sense the uncertainty that now sat behind his eyes.

'It's no secret,' he began slowly, one hand rubbing his chin lightly, 'it's no secret that of everyone in the family I'm the one who ... How shall I put this? I have a very different, a particular way of looking at the world that is not exactly in keeping with the way, let's say ... my brother Sandro views it, or your Nonna, or maybe – but less so – your mama ... I haven't always done the expected ... I mean ...' Zio Paul paused and cocked his head to look at me more closely. Then he grinned. 'My view is that if what's expected is ... is ... if what's expected satisfies what you want, then fine, do as is expected. If not, then maybe you have to do what you want and take your chances.'

My uncle had never spoken to me like this before. This was all too serious coming from the man I knew liked nothing better than to agitate a situation just for the sake of a laugh. I wasn't sure whether he was trying to explain something to me or confessing. Embarrassed, I coughed. My uncle pinched the end of his nose and narrowed his eyes.

'Dottore,' he began again, more confidently, 'if I told you that there was a ... a certain – '

'OH JESU ... OH JESU ... TONY ... TONY ... *COS È SUCCESSO* ... ?'

Zia Graziella's voice cut through the sense of understanding that had begun to settle around Zio Paul and me. Her shriek filled the back yard.

'SANDRO ... *VIENI* ... QUICK ... SANDRO ... OH DIO ... OH JESU, TONY ... TONY!!'

We must all have jumped at once, for in that instant there was a mad rush for the back gate, with Zia Graziella leading the charge, Nonna in her wake, and my mum and dad on her heels. Between them rushed Machiavelli, a morsel of sausage hanging from his mouth as he tried to eat and run at the same time. As he pushed past me I heard him whisper under his breath in his clearest Italian, 'God, give me strength to tolerate this woman.'

And then they were gone, spilling out into the park next to the house and toppling over each other in an effort to reach Zio Sandro's son, who had crashed my bike head first into a lightpole in the park.

'I hope he hasn't caused too much damage,' Zio Paul said as seriously as he could when it became obvious that Zia Graziella had overreacted as usual. 'I've heard that lightpoles are expensive to repair.'

5

From what I'd heard about holidays, routine was a dirty word. Days lapsed into one another and if you wanted to stay up for the entire holiday you could; on holiday anything was possible, or at the very least it should have been. I thought of this as we crossed the bridge at San Remo, two hours behind schedule because Mr Valdo had taken a wrong turn at Tooradin.

'You'd think the man would know the way,' Dad scoffed yet again. He rolled his head from side to side and tried to keep up with the Valdos' pale-blue Datsun. 'The man drives like a woman.' A moment later he added, 'Maybe that's why they don't have children. They're both women.'

It was meant as a joke but Mum spat back, 'That must explain your brother then.'

Dad stiffened visibly, 'It's not Frank, woman, it's Gina. He lowered his voice, for the sake of Rose and me I guess. 'She's an empty vessel.'

'They suit each other then,' Mum whispered. She gazed out the window again. 'Empty vessel and empty head.'

I wasn't about to buy into their argument. I wanted to

take in as much as I could from my first sighting of the island. When the time came to tell the boys back at St Joe's about my holiday I wanted to have all the details ready at hand. I'd studied the maps and brochures Mr Valdo had given us very carefully and now I identified everything I could from them: the trawlers moored to the jetty by the bridge, the markers out in the Narrows, the early-morning sun shimmering across the water's surface, and the scraggy vegetation that choked the fringes of the island. I tried to sear all of these images into my memory.

Even the cawing of the seagulls hovering like animated kites in an air stiff with a cool sea breeze sang musically in my ears. Of course I'd seen seagulls before, but they weren't like these island birds, which weren't trapped, locked in by land, bound to place by familiarity and convenience.

This *was* a different world. The land was not of black earth, but of dirty-gold sand, a muted yellow that held heat within itself. To look at it, as the land spread out in dunes and hillocks to my left and flat pastures to my right, I could almost believe we – the Martinesis – were a part of it all; neither strangers nor newcomers.

By the time we turned into the camping ground I'd ceased being surprised by the sights: houses on stilts with steep steps climbing into forever; pockets of ramshackle tents behind sand dunes where skinny, long-haired men played cricket with eskies for wickets, and dogs chased every loose ball; the grey–blue birds whose strange call rose and fell at every turn of the road. My surprise had been replaced by a kind of quiet disbelief that the Martinesi clan were actually anywhere other than at home.

I wondered whether I'd suddenly wake up and find that I'd only been dreaming. Under my breath I said a well-rehearsed prayer to the Blessed Mother that, for the time being at least, She allow this dream to go on.

A sign on a giant steel lattice arch that stretched across the gravel driveway to the camping ground read: Penguin Rock Caravan Park. Below it was a smaller, less elaborate sign: Tow your own or stay in one of ours. Children and dogs welcome.

'What a relief,' I sneered at Rose as I leaned across Nonna, 'they allow children and sisters.'

Rose screwed up her eyes, looked out at the sign, then back at me.

'Ma,' she cried, but already we were under the arch and pulling up alongside the Valdos.

Dad wound down his window. The car was flooded with the crisp smell of air fresh off a cold surf and the muted stirrings of invisible creatures in the trees that surrounded us. I breathed deeply, letting the tingle of overnight dew wash over me.

We waited while Mr Valdo brought the manager to our car and introduced us each in turn.

Mr Andrews was a tall light-haired man with long bony arms and muscular legs whose feet were pushed into multi-coloured thongs.

'You've got the same spot as last year, Peter,' he said, casting a searching eye over our car.

'Onedaful, Mr Andrews,' Mr Valdo cooed, shaking hands, before jumping into his car and signalling for us to follow him.

Nonna, who Mum had thought would enjoy some time with us as a family, made her farting sound and clutched her handbag tightly to her lap.

Rose and I looked at her.

'What's wrong?' Rose asked.

Nonna drew her head back, closed her eyes and exhaled

loudly. 'Did you see those girls on their own?' she answered through pressed lips. 'Barely daylight and already they're wandering around like street urchins.'

'I doubt you'll see many street urchins, as you call them, here,' Mum cut in, and before she could continue Dad added, 'A few no-hopers maybe. Lazy good-for-nothings, yes ... but street urchins no ... Although, with a town by the name of Cowes you might find a stray calf or two.'

Dad slapped his hands on the steering wheel, taken by his own joke. This was how I liked Dad – jovial, good-natured, a hard-working family man. That other man, that man who had stood with his back to me at Fernando's, was not my father at all I wanted to convince myself. He was an imposter out there for the benefit of Giuseppe Dellavecchia.

Our camp site was on the blind side of the shower and toilet block, a dull brown-brick rectangular building set on a thick bed of concrete any self-respecting Italian concreter would have been proud of.

'Smells like a toilet brush left too long in the sun,' Nonna observed with a terse shake of her head.

'At least we know it's clean,' I said, hoping Dad hadn't heard her. It wouldn't take much for him to head us all back to Melbourne again.

'Never trust a house where all the rooms smell like a toilet. You can be sure either the toilet is too clean, or the smell is there to disguise a greater mess.'

Great, I thought, we're here for one minute and already Nonna's started on the riddles.

To everyone's amazement – not least of all mine – Dad, Mr Valdo, Rose and I actually managed to erect the tent with only minor hitches. By about noon we had it up and filled to bursting with all manner of indispensable camping gear.

'Do people at these places always stand about and stare?' my mother asked Mrs Valdo.

'Only when they want a laugh,' Rose interjected, smirking, but no one paid her any attention.

'I recognise some of the faces,' Mrs Valdo replied. 'Some of them helped us put our tent up last year. Perhaps they just gathered to see if they could help.'

'More like they gathered to see if we'd manage,' Rose said. She was already annoyed because Mum wouldn't let her go exploring the camping ground on her own, insisting that Nonna accompany her.

'I'll go with her,' I volunteered, then added, 'with Rose, that is.'

Mum looked at us. 'Maybe after lunch,' she said.

'Let them go, Teresa. They're safer here than in their own back yard.' Mum looked at Mrs Valdo as if to say: How would you know? and then begrudgingly gave in. 'But only for . . .' She consulted her watch, 'half an hour, then I want you both back. Davide, you understand?'

Rose and I turned on our heels and ran back towards the entrance and what we figured was the games room and kiosk area Mr Valdo had told us about. Out of sight of our camp site we slowed to a jog and then a slow walk. Around us, behind, between and in a few cases almost on top of the gum trees, stood caravans, trailervans and tents. Some were permanent fixtures, surrounded by little gardens and defined with annexes, awnings, fixed swing-chairs and, by one caravan, even a bird bath complete with running water.

Rose and I looked at each other.

There were half-naked people everywhere, some in clusters around barbecues, some reclined whale-like in too-small banana lounges, others at fold-out tables, and others still in canvas doorways looking for all the world like outback squatters. I felt as if I was walking through an alien landscape.

'It's like lunch time at school,' Rose observed casually. 'Only much more civilised.'

By the time we reached the office building, which we could see housed the games room, kiosk and undersized TV room, both Rose and I had been bitten raw by swarms of angry, blood-thirsty mosquitoes that tailed us relentlessly.

'Bloody things,' I snapped, swatting and waving, desperate to scratch every bite.

Rose went ahead of me into the games room and I would have followed had it not been for the voice that boomed at my back.

'YOU,' it called.

I was scratching my ankles, and for a moment I didn't look round; after all, no one knew me.

'Don't act as though you didn't hear me, son. Stand up straight and tall.'

I glanced back between my knees. It was Mr Andrews and he was standing right behind me, arms folded. I stood up and faced him.

'Me?' I mouthed innocently.

'What does that sign over there say?' Mr Andrews asked, pointing over the top of my head.

I looked behind me. On the wall by the office door was a sign: *The Andrews' Rules and Regulations for the Keeping of the PEACE.* Under that wording were a number of itemised points, including: Do not enter Games Room, TV Room, or Kiosk with bare feet; Never be the last one out of the Games Room or TV Room and forget to switch the lights off; Replace any and all equipment you have used back WHERE IT BELONGS; Compromise over TV Channel selections otherwise TURN IT OFF; and second from the bottom, DO NOT CURSE, BLASPHEME OR SWEAR.

Rose stepped out under the veranda and blocked my view so I turned back to Mr Andrews.

'The word "bloody" is offensive and inappropriate,' he began the moment our eyes met. 'Another violation of the rules like that and you'll be barred from this area until I see fit to let you return.' He walked off, peeping into the games room as he went.

I stood where I was. I couldn't believe it. Here I was, miles and miles from school and I'd just been visited by the ghost of Brother Ignatius. I just couldn't believe it.

When I regained my composure I realised people were staring at me. Stay-at-home, stay-at-home, their faces were saying. And who could blame them? On holiday for five minutes and already I'd made an idiot of myself.

'C'mon,' I said to Rose, 'we'll come back later.' I led the way at a trot back towards our tent, the sun blazing down savagely on my naked head.

When we got back to the tent Mr Valdo suggested we eat quickly, then head down to the beach. I was rapt. We didn't get to swim often, Rose and I. Mum and Dad were paranoid about sharks and jellyfish – and about us being exposed to what Mum said were drunken men and women in various stages of undress, so we waited for Mum to react. She looked at her workmate, who smiled serenely.

'But only if you both help us clean up after lunch,' Mum said finally, her eyes meeting ours, but only briefly.

'Yeaass!' I cried, perhaps too vigorously, for Dad gave me one of his evil eyes. 'Si, Mama,' I said much more softly, and the evil eye melted away.

As it happened, our idea of what a beach was and what Mr

Valdo thought it meant were two very different things.

'Mum, there's nothing here but seaweed and rocks!'

Rose was almost right. The 'beach' Mr Valdo took us to was full of seaweed and rocks, but something else too. It was surrounded by towering cliffs over which gulls struggled to stay airborne against the blustering wind.

'Maybe we can all just throw ourselves into the whitecaps,' I said loudly so that Mr Valdo would hear, and I pointed out to anyone who cared to listen that it was a well-known fact that sharks wouldn't swim in amongst crashing waves, so at least we'd all be safe from being eaten alive. 'And besides, even if Nonna can't swim, the waves can smash her back to the sand.'

Mr Valdo laughed at this observation and shook his head at me. 'No, Davide, this water not for swim. Too much dangerous. Look it how the water she crashes on the rocks.'

I made as though to crane my neck for a closer look over the precipice where we stood. Rose came up beside me. 'I don't know. There's a spot just there,' I whispered through clenched teeth. 'See, only a handful of rocks and a mere tidal wave.'

If I hadn't jumped back my mother would have had my ear off she grabbed it that hard. When she let it go it throbbed. 'Very nice, Pietro,' she observed rather sourly, giving me a look that said, 'not another word or next time you *will* lose your ear'.

Mr Valdo appeared satisfied with this reassurance from my mother and led our expedition down a rickety flight of wooden stairs where Nonna and Dad grimaced at the biting wind. 'This is called Storm Bay', Mr Valdo explained in Italian for Nonna's benefit. 'The other beaches are too crowded with kids and loud music. Too much ompa-ompa-ompa.'

'Oh yeah, the old ompa-ompa!' I said to no one in particular. 'We wouldn't want to get caught among the ompa-ompa. You never know what exposure to music, laughter and the water all in one hit can do to you.' Rose whispered something about there needing to be a rest home somewhere nearby for people like the Valdos, and Dad coughed too casually.

'It's beautiful here,' Mrs Valdo enthused, going off ahead as though to emphasise her statement. 'So peaceful. Pietro and I always come here to get kelp and mussels. Last year we came here almost every day. We even had a picnic down on the sand.'

'This isn't a beach,' my father hissed at my mother as he pushed past her. 'This is one of those places where old ships come to die.'

Mum wouldn't be drawn and after closing her eyes as though to gather her thoughts, nodded that Rose and I should follow the others down the steps.

'C'mon,' called Mrs Valdo, who had come back to give Nonna a hand over the rocks. 'I show you what they call Pyramid Rock. Come.' Nonna complained that she didn't have the right shoes for this sort of activity, but Mrs Valdo led her between a pile of rounded rocks, encouraging her with soft murmurs of appreciation for her every tentative step.

'C'mon, Nonna, you can do it. Scale the heights! Go for it!' I called after her. 'What's a few rocks to an old woman suffering from swollen legs and water on the knee!' When my father turned his evil eye on me I shrugged my shoulders. 'A joke,' I whispered. 'She hasn't really got water on the knee.' Then more softly, for Rose's ear, I added, 'She's got it on the brain like the rest of us.'

And so our caravan of would-be explorers went forward,

Rose and me taking up the rear, stumbling over rocks, scratching ourselves against overhangs, and ducking the seagulls that swooped in low on bursts of frigid currents.

'If we're real lucky,' mused Rose just loud enough for our mother to glance back and glare at us, 'we could come back tomorrow and take turns feeding food scraps to the seagulls.'

'Better still, we could come back and throw ourselves over the cliffs onto a ledge and test if the rescue service here is as good as they say it is,' I replied. 'Or maybe ... I know, maybe we can get Machiavelli out here and have him tell us to our faces just how stupid we are.'

Rose laughed.

'Don't laugh, Rose,' I said with mock seriousness. 'This is serious shit. These people really believe this is a beach. I reckon they really believe this is fun. You're having fun, aren't you? I mean, look out there, it's water isn't it? You can't swim in it, but you sure as shit can drown in it!'

To say I almost choked at the realisation that this was to be my initiation into the beach-mode of holidaying is to make light – very light – of my impulse to throw Mr Valdo and his dear wife out into Bass Strait. Nathan and the others were right; we wogs were useless outside of our neat environment of garlic cloves, pasta dura bread, soccer and opera.

Maybe Zio Paul had been wrong. Maybe we weren't cut out to look beyond our front doors.

6

'Now, don't any of you say a word about today other than
"it was fun",' Mum said when we pulled up beside our tent.
She turned and looked hard at me, but even in the dim
light I could see she was disappointed for Rose and me –
and Dad.

'Maybe tomorrow, eh,' she whispered, then to Dad, 'and
you, don't you start again about nearly breaking your leg. It
was your own stupid fault for chasing that bird.'

I saw Dad stiffen in his seat.

Mr Valdo came over, a broad grin on his face, happy to
have his two bags full of mussels. He glanced into the back
seat and nodded.

'Tomorrow I know a very good place to take the kids. But
we leave for a surprise, okay,' he crooned. Then he slapped
the roof of the car playfully and strode off with an invitation
for a late supper.

'I hope those mussels give him food poisoning,' I muttered,
and stalked out to the toilet block.

I couldn't believe that I'd spent an entire day, one entire
day of my precious three-day holiday, searching for mussels

and kelp along a wind-swept beach where the only things in the water were fish, and surfies too sun-struck to appreciate the dangers of the turbulent water.

'Got a light, mate?'

The suddenness of the voice in the dull light of the toilets caught me by surprise. I stepped back from the urinal, splashing my ankles.

Whoever it was behind me laughed. I finished quickly, too quickly, and felt the last drops trickle into my pants.

'Shit,' I mumbled.

'Got a light?' The voice was sharper now, more demanding.

I turned to face the speaker. It was a kid of about my age, and he was standing in one of the open cubicles, cigarette in hand, legs crossed at the ankles. When I looked at him he held the cigarette up, waving it at me.

'Forgot me lighter,' he said.

I shrugged my shoulders and held my hands out palms up.

The smoker snorted, scratched his forehead and pocketed the cigarette. 'Can you get a box of matches maybe?' he asked.

I shook my head and he stepped forward.

'You've pissed all over your feet, mate,' he observed with a wry laugh. 'I'd wash it off, otherwise you'll be covered in bull ants by morning.'

I nodded and moved off, embarrassed, and splashed water over my feet from a tap by the entrance.

The would-be smoker stood watching me. He had stepped out into the light and I saw that he was holding a big texta in his other hand. He must have noticed me staring at it because he slipped it into his pocket.

'What you don't see . . .' he said, and I knew that I'd interrupted him and he wasn't impressed.

When I turned to go he moved forward, barring my way. 'Haven't seen you around before,' he said slowly. 'Whatsyaname?'

I thought of Nathan and how he took pleasure in intimidating the new kids at school. I knew it was best to answer simply and directly.

'David.'

This seemed to amuse him and he repeated my name as though it were a chant: Da-vid, Da-vid, Da-vid. 'Whatareya doing here, Da-vid?' he asked.

I thought it had been obvious, but I nodded towards the urinal just the same.

'I know you had a piss. You're not related to Andrews, are ya?' The kid moved a fraction closer and narrowed his eyes. 'I bet you didn't even need a piss. I bet Andrews made you come in here to check up on me, eh.'

I saw his fists clench and open again slowly. He followed my eyes, then grinned. 'Andrews has this thing about me, right,' he went on. 'He thinks I'm always getting in where I don't belong. Like here for instance.' He pointed a finger at me. 'Andrews is a ballbreaker. Never gives up. Thinks because he owns this place he can tell everyone what to do . . . Even you.'

I flinched and the kid cocked his head. 'I saw him get stuck into ya by the office,' he grinned. 'Gave you a real once over, eh. He hates swearin'. He's got this thing about swearin'. Swearin' and rootin'. Reckons if you root before you're married some god or other is gonna make ya dick fall off. Shit, I reckon me brother must have gone through about ten or twelve dicks by now.' When the kid laughed his eyes remained open, looking right at me, as though daring me not to laugh. I gave a snort.

'I don't even know Mr Andrews.'

The kid sniffed loudly, walked around me and, leaning against the wall, his face in shadows, said, 'You wouldn't try to put one over me wouldya? Whatsyaname again?'

'David,' I replied and stepped away. I almost expected to feel a tug on my arm or a hand on my shoulder. When it didn't come I walked briskly out into the night and was almost at our tent when I heard my name being called softly.

'Da-a-avid, Da-a-avid, won't you come out to play?' The hollow, mocking voice chilled me the way the sight of Nathan and his hangers-on always chilled me when they suddenly appeared round a corner at school, all grins and waving arms.

'Da-vid, be a mate and get us a light, eh.'

There was a lump, cold and hard as ice, in my belly. There was no way I was going to get him a light. In fact I didn't venture out of the tent again at all that first night. And when the light we'd hooked up in the tent suddenly went out about half an hour after I got back from the toilet, I didn't have to think twice to figure out who had probably pulled the lead from the meter-box.

The next morning I was still yawning into my breakfast, bleary eyed and light-headed from a restless night of hearing sounds that most probably weren't there, when Mrs Valdo burst into the tent.

'Teresa,' she said in a tinny, trembling voice, *'vieni fiori.'*

Mum stopped plaiting Rose's hair, asked Nonna to take over, and went outside. I craned my neck forward but still couldn't hear what Mrs Valdo was saying. They went round to the rear of the tent, their shadows faint against the canvas.

Moments later Mum was at the door again. Her eyes flared.

'Ma? What is it?' I asked.

'Davide, *vieni*. Come here. Now.'

'What's the problem, Ma?' Rose asked, flinching under Nonna's hands.

'You just get your hair done,' Mum snapped.

Rose and I looked at each other and I followed Mum out to the rear of the tent.

'David,' Mrs Valdo said, her voice wobbling. She pointed to the tent's rear panel. In large black capital letters someone had scrawled my name.

My jaw dropped. I found myself looking from the letters that made up my name to Mum and Mrs Valdo in turn.

'What is this?' my mother asked in a manner that didn't demand a reply.

I fumbled for words, blinked stupidly at the carefully written letters.

'What does this mean, Davide?' Mum asked again.

What could I say? Didn't she know I hadn't written it? Of course she did, I told myself.

'I . . . I dunno,' I replied.

'But it's your name.'

I couldn't deny that.

Mrs Valdo buried her mouth in her hand. 'How could this happen?' she asked. 'Why?'

I was about to say that I knew who might be responsible but I held my tongue. Who knew what trouble I'd be buying into if I pointed the finger at that kid.

'I reckon it's just kids playing a stupid joke,' I mumbled. 'I . . . I bet someone heard my name, followed me here, saw this was our tent, and for a bit of a laugh decided to do this. And I bet they also pulled the power on us last night.'

'What!' snapped Mrs Valdo. 'Joke! This not a joke. What kind of joke is this, Davide? This is not a joke. This doesn't make me want to laugh.' She waved her hands in the air, stirring the morning stillness. 'Someone here has purposely damaged my property and I want to know who. I want to know why. Why? What have I done to deserve this? What? I want whoever is responsible for this caught and made to pay to have this cleaned.'

Mrs Valdo stormed off. When I turned to follow, my mother reached out and stopped me. 'Davide, you have no idea who did this – or why?' she asked, her eyes still and prying.

I gave a slight shrug and her grip fell away. 'Come on, Ma,' I said, my voice thin. 'Why should I know anything about this? I mean, it's not as though I've been here long enough to have made enemies or anything.'

Mum glared at me. 'But it's your name, Davide. Why?'

'Search me,' I answered, careful not to let my eyes stray too far from hers. 'I'll get some water and soap and see if I can get it off.'

I found myself wondering what Nathan might have said or done in my place. Doubtless he wouldn't have let on that he knew. He would have dealt with the matter first-hand. That was Nathan's way. But who was I kidding? I asked myself. I might not let on about the kid in the toilets, but it wasn't because I wanted to confront him myself.

'What do you think Papa will say?' my mother called after me as I strode away. I shrugged but didn't look back.

By the time Mr Andrews finally came to inspect the damage, Dad and Mr Valdo were back from their luckless early-morning fishing expedition and were carefully inspecting the marks I'd tried to remove.

Mr Andrews's first words on seeing me were, 'Oh, it's you is it.' And then, before anyone could even begin to tell him about the vandalism, Mr Andrews went off about my foul-mouthed outburst outside the games room. 'We have a certain standard of behaviour here that we expect everyone to abide by. Dirty language is certainly not part of the standard we like to uphold. That's the language of louts and hooligans.'

Dad gave me one of his evil eyes and shifted his weight. He hadn't expected this news about his own son, and I could see the veins in his neck bulging.

'I'm real sorry about what I said,' I offered, 'but I guess what Mr Valdo really wants to know is, what's going to be done about this vandalism?'

I preferred not to look directly at my father, and especially not when Mr Andrews surprised us all by asking, 'Has David ever been in any serious trouble before?'

I'm not sure who spoke first, my mum or my dad, but Dad's voice cut across all else.

'What for you talk all this bullshit? What got to do if my son David him been trouble or no?'

'I'm wondering, that's all, why of all the names available to him . . .' Mr Andrews began.

'Or her,' Rose cut in.

Mr Andrews ignored her. 'This isn't the only tent vandalised you realise. Altogether there are at least eight tents or caravans with your son's name scrawled on them. I just have to ask myself, why his name? Why not Simon, or Paul, or . . . or . . .'

There was a giggle. It was Rose. 'Good one,' she laughed. 'Now you're a *vandal* too, Big Brother.'

I didn't see any reason to laugh. I shrugged my shoulders at Mum, then Dad.

'Wot,' Mum said in a whisper. 'Him tink David do dis tings?'

'I'm not saying that, exactly,' Mr Andrews said, when Mum asked the same question of Dad in Italian and Dad's face darkened. 'All I'm suggesting is that maybe your son has been keeping bad company and this is the result of some – I don't know exactly – some feud perhaps ... some ...'

Dad stepped up to Mr Andrews and eye-balled him. 'You not talk no more like this,' he exploded. 'I'm tell you now, my son him *here* with me when our light go out. David was here with me and that you must believe because I am a father and I don like see my son get hisself accuse of something him no done!' Dad drew a breath. 'It don matter to you bloody peoples how hard we dago bastard work, still you not got one good word say for us. Still you like say we thief and crook and no-good wogs. What for? What for you can only think bad for us?' He was steaming now, his face a deep red.

I swallowed hard and watched Dad point his finger at the ground, boring into it with his anger. Beside Dad, Mr Valdo had gone a deathly white, blinking blindly into space while his wife clung to Mum and Nonna alternatively. Rose looked on as though she were miles away.

Dad reached out and put his arm about my shoulders, locking me to him. 'Just because my son him name David, does not mean he done damage to those people's property ... So now I say, no more talk about David,' he seethed. 'If he sweared you did okay to tell him off.' He tightened his hold on me and I knew that later I'd have to answer to that charge. 'But never ever again do you come to me and say my son him done what you now want say to me him done. *Never. Mai ... Finito e basta.*'

No one stirred, not even Mr Andrews. I wanted to vanish, but I was trapped where I stood.

It was Mr Andrews who finally broke the silence. He looked back and forth from Dad to Mr Valdo. 'I didn't intend to offend you Mr – '

'Martinesi,' Rose informed him glibly.

'Mr Martinesi, thank you. I guess I will have to accept your word that your son David was with you last night when all this ... this mayhem happened. You must admit, however, that it is strange that of all the names to choose our invisible culprit chose one to which only your son answers.'

'No stranger than to believe that a vandal would leave his own given name as a signature to his crime, or that he would deface his own tent,' my Nonna said suddenly so that we all turned to look at her. She was standing with her hands clasped together, her back arched slightly away from the circle of activity, her eyes alert. I was now more convinced than ever that, when it came to English, my Nonna had selective understanding.

'I beg your pardon?' asked Mr Andrews, and Rose translated into English what Nonna had said.

After some hesitation Mr Valdo persuaded Dad and Mr Andrews to shake hands. Dad made me apologise for swearing and assured Mr Andrews that the next time I swore he'd cut off my tongue – an assurance that seemed to distress Mr Andrews.

When Mr Andrews had left our tent and Dad had cooled down enough to hear Mum out, it was decided that this was where the matter would rest. No more was to be said about it, not now, not when the holiday was over, not ever.

'Yeah,' piped up Rose with a sly wink in my direction. 'You wouldn't want to spoil the holiday spirit.'

As I waited for my dad to lift his hand and dismiss me I looked up, and I saw that he was staring directly at me, his eyes brimming with tears.

7

I did get to swim in salt water after all! Mr Valdo eventually ran out of sights to show us, although he had made one mighty last effort to try and convince Mum and Dad that Rose and I would probably like to see the seals out on Seal Rock.

Rose and I were ready to go in an instant; the rest of them were deathly slow. Between packing a lunch big enough to feed the entire population of the island, and deciding whether or not to bring along the card table, the oldies wasted away a good hour and a half chasing their tails around the tent. And when it seemed like we were finally ready to hit the waves, Nonna decided she had better go to the toilet before we left because at least she had grown accustomed to the smells of these ones. That saw another half-hour slip away.

'Got your bathers on, Nonna?' Rose asked cheekily when Nonna edged in next to her in the back seat of the car.

'You can laugh,' Nonna said, 'but when I was young I really was something to look at.'

'Yeah,' smirked Dad. 'Just the kind of thing your father needed to keep the crows from the corn crop!' When Dad laughed I saw Mum grin despite herself. 'You're so heartless sometimes,' she said, but there was no malice in her voice and Dad turned out of the camping ground behind the Valdos, his long flat laugh ringing in my ears.

It seemed that like me, Mum and Dad had put the business of the tent and Mr Andrews aside, and I was glad of that. What with still half expecting Nathan to show up, and not knowing what the kid from the toilet might do next, I wanted desperately to believe nothing more could go wrong with this trip.

'So, this is the Cowes beach,' Dad observed as we unloaded the cargo of gear from the boot. Traditional Greek music blared out from across the lawns where a group of guys and girls kicked a soccer ball around. 'Hear that?' he asked me. 'That music is almost as good as ours. Much better anyway than you young people's rubbish music.' Dad pursed his lips and broke into English. 'Blah ... Blah ... I'm luv yu so-o mush I can go crazy ... Rock ... Rock ... Oh yeah, rock ... Bloody bullshit music.'

I smiled but made no reply. I didn't want to spoil the mood. I didn't want anything reminding Dad of the day before.

Like all good Italians on a mission, Rose had gone ahead with Nonna to find just the right spot to lay down our load. It had to have shade, but not be too cool, because Nonna suffered when it was damp. It had to have easy access to the toilet. It had to have a view of the water. It had to be within sight of the car in case there was a torrential downpour and we had to run for cover. And it had to be a spot where Rose and I would be suitably hidden when it came time to have lunch so that we wouldn't be stared at when the year's supply of food came pouring out.

'Ma,' I said, dropping the last of the blankets necessary

for the post-lunch snooze, 'you coming in or what? The water's supposed to be nice and warm here.'

Mum tossed her head back, her hair flying away behind her in the breeze. When she smiled she looked more relaxed than she had in a very long time. 'Me? Maybe just to wet my feet.'

I knew that although we had made it as far as the beach itself, getting into the water was another matter again. There was no way Mum and Dad would let Rose or me go anywhere near the water unless one of them was there to supervise. I knew that if I argued I would be banned from the water completely. The best option was the course of least resistance: invite Mum in as well.

'Nonna, what're you doing?' Rose asked, alarmed.

I looked across and there was Nonna hitching her dress up over her knees, and attempting to knot it into makeshift shorts.

'This is a good dress,' Nonna snapped. 'What for I should get it ruined?'

It was in these sorts of moments that Rose and I looked at one another and prayed for the ground to swallow us up. Still, it wasn't as bad as expected, for when we finally got to the water's edge, Nonna's bathers were probably the least embarrassing of the spur-of-the-moment costumes.

'Must be a kind of ritual,' I whispered to Rose. 'You gather all the old farts in the one place, get them to dress like clowns, and then crowd them along the beach to scare off the sharks.'

'It's kinda cute,' Rose replied and smiled back toward where Nonna hobbled behind us along the scorching sand in her open-toed sandals. 'I bet in all the years she's lived in Australia Nonna's probably only ever been to the beach three or four times.'

I watched Nonna as she came through the throng, stepping over discarded towels, pushing past groups of kids, and finally stopping at the water's edge. She looked so utterly out of her element that I almost wanted to race her back to the tent and hide her safely away. Almost.

'Can you believe this, Rose,' I said instead. 'Us, the Martinesi family, here at Cowes. Not St Kilda Beach. Not Elwood Beach. Not Port Melbourne, but Cowes. Cowes, Phillip Island.'

At that moment the world was a great place to be. The salt water, when I lunged into it, was so wonderfully alive and sharp with the tang of seaweed and sand that I couldn't have cared less if Nathan himself had come ambling up the beach and spotted me out in the crowd. I even found myself kind of willing Nathan to turn up. It was becoming clear that a communication of sorts had sprung up between us. Not a direct communication really, because somehow or other it involved Ralph. Odd as it seemed, Ralph was as much a part of my growing friendship with Nathan as was my shifting status from stay-at-home to novice holiday-goer.

We were not long back from the beach when Mr Valdo and Dad decided they would try their luck fishing for calamari off the jetty. They asked Mum and Mrs Valdo to join them, but Nonna wasn't feeling too well, so Mum and Mrs Valdo thought it best they help her get an early night. When I declined the offer too, Rose persuaded them to take her along instead. She didn't feel the need to fuss over Nonna and another of her dizzy spells.

Dad snorted and fixed the evil eye on me. 'Your sister wants to come, why not you?'

'I just don't feel like it, Dad, sorry. I'm stuffed. I just want to hang around here, that's all.'

Rose, who knew Dad was uncomfortable about taking his daughter fishing, came to my rescue. 'David couldn't catch a drop of water in a rain storm, Papa. Besides, you know how much better I am at sitting still for a long time. David gets all nervy and starts to move about so much he scares off the fish.'

'He can learn to be patient,' Dad said, still hoping that I would change my mind. 'Fishing is good for the soul. It's primitive. Like eating. A boy can learn a lot just by sitting silently and listening to nothing in particular.'

'So can a girl, Dad.' Rose looked at me as if daring me to ruin it for her. 'Right, David?'

'Dad, Rose is right. I'd just be in the way. I'm too tired. I reckon I got a bit too much sun.'

'You can say that again,' said Rose, then to Dad, 'If you don't want me to come just tell me, Dad, and I'll go make a bed, or bake a pizza or something.'

I just wanted to be alone with my thoughts. It was as simple as that. I sauntered around the quiet of the camping ground for a while then headed back to the tent. I could hear Nonna starting one of her favourite discussions: the fall from grace of those families who let their children run wild. I decided to drop in on our neighbours.

Our camp-site neighbours were a young couple with two little boys who were always running to Rose for attention. I'd got to know them all well enough to be able to wander across and sit with them.

That night though, they weren't in. Their tent was zippered shut, their deck-chairs and fold-out card table neatly stacked inside, and their car was not in its usual spot. I don't know what I was looking for, if anything, but I found myself running my eyes over their site.

'You won't find anything of value there, Da-vid.'

The voice jumped out of the shadows at me and I recoiled as though from a rifle blast. I stumbled against a guy rope and fell on my back. Laughter ruffled the air.

I struggled to get to my feet and took a few paces back, searching the line of scrub for the source of the laughter. A small flash of matchlight burst amongst the shadows, and I saw the kid from the night before.

'They ain't got nothin' worth takin',' he informed me coldly.

I wanted to tell him that I had no intention of taking anything anyway so –

'Listen, Da-vid,' the vandal said softly, cutting my thoughts off, 'I appreciate you not lettin' on about me to Andrews and the rest, you know. I sorta knew you wouldn't but I wasn't sure.' He crossed the short space between us and came to stand almost toe to toe with me. In the sparse light he was all angles and sharp edges, large and threatening.

'Smoke?' he asked right into my face.

I blinked hard and drew my head back. 'No.'

The smoker nodded wryly then looked over his shoulder at the padlocked tent.

'If you want I can cut us in,' he announced, producing a flick-knife. The blade hissed as it left its sheath and winked in the moonlight. 'I can tell you now though, it ain't worth wastin' our time, unless of course you like toys and shit like that. That's about all they got.'

My eyes locked on the blade, held by its silver sheen. I shifted my weight from foot to foot and the kid shook his head dismissively.

'I ain't gonna cut you,' he growled, retracting the blade.

I could hear my heart slap at my chest, my ears filled with thunder, and I tasted bile.

'This is Bluebeard,' he said, holding the knife out for me

to examine. When I didn't make a move Bluebeard's owner grinned expansively and added, 'Pity you ain't stayin' for the New Year's Eve do tomorra night. It's the only decent time of the year here. The rest of the time we just have to make do with the crappy games room, maybe a ride into Cowes if we're lucky . . .' His voice trailed off and he drew heavily on his cigarette.

'So, do you like the place or what?' he asked stiffly. 'Most people reckon it's all right. Ain't much to do here at night though. Bit of a shit pit really. Not like in Cowes.' He looked up at me. 'You been to Cowes, right?'

I nodded.

'Cowes is all right for a bit of a laugh I guess. At least a guy can move about without havin' a fence to lock him in.' He took the cigarette from his mouth and examined it closely. 'The beach is pretty tame but – at Cowes I mean. For really good surf, for a bit of sport, you gotta get to Sunderland Bay or Woolamai . . . You been to Wooli?'

'No,' I answered through a croak.

'Top beach, no shit. Heaps and heaps of white-caps. And breakers like you wouldn't believe. Do you surf, David?'

I shook my head.

'Didn't think so. Not many of you blow-ins do. Your mob are more into sun worshippin' and walkin' up and down along the beach showin' off your hairy chests and even hairier backs.' He laughed, 'And that's just the women! By the way, does your sis have a better mo' than your old man?' He laughed hard, shaking his head as though to clear it of the unbearable hilarity of his comments.

'So, you gonna sit down or wait to be knocked down?' he asked sharply a moment later.

I sat down.

We didn't say a word for several long minutes. Bluebeard's

owner finished off his cigarette slowly, as though I was not even there. I watched him, unsure of what he wanted.

A question quietly pushed itself out of my mouth. 'Why did you scrawl my name all over the place?'

That same sniggering laugh I'd heard before from the invisibility of the shadows came at me again.

'I thought it was kinda funny meself,' the kid sniggered.

'Yeah, well maybe, but Andrews isn't convinced I didn't do it.'

'I told you.' The kid snapped his eyes and turned on me angrily. 'Don't worry about him. He ain't gonna do nothin'. He never does, you got that. You understand, wog?'

'I'm not a wog.'

'You're a dago then, same difference.'

I wanted to get up and leave but I didn't. Besides, where was I going to go – back to the tent and Nonna's sermon? I preferred to stay where I was, secure in the knowledge that if things got out of hand a shout would doubtless bring Mum running. I wondered what Nathan would have thought of my gutlessness, and what he'd have thought of this weedy-looking kid sitting with his knees pulled up to his chest.

'This place stinks, doesn't it. Same faces year in, year out. Same people in the same caravans. Same tents and cars and motorbikes.' The kid paused and looked at me. 'It's enough to make you puke sometimes.' He paused again, then asked, 'Ever smoked a joint?'

A joint? Was he kidding?

'Ever seen a woman naked?' he asked next. 'And I don't mean in a magazine, either.'

When I whispered that it was no big deal, Bluebeard's owner gave one of his hoarse laughs. 'No big deal. You serious?' When he'd stopped laughing he shook his head at me.

'You ain't a poof are ya? I mean you ain't – you know, AC-DC maybe?'

AC-DC?

'AC-DC,' he shrugged, 'You know, a bit each way – Arthur *and* Martha. Get it?'

I got it. 'No, I'm not – AC-DC. And I'm not gay.'

Bluebeard's owner dropped to his knees and stared me straight in the eyes.

'So if you ain't a poof and you ain't a bit each way, how come you've never seen a woman naked?' he sneered.

What did he want me to say? What was he expecting me to do?

'I bet you go to one of them fancy posh schools with no girls, eh,' he went on. 'Just boys. Room after room of boys. And not a girl in sight. Yeah, I bet that's why you've never seen a girl naked, because they're not allowed to hang around, eh. I bet you guys all shower together and sneak peeks at each other's dicks.'

I opened my mouth to protest but the kid had ceased talking and was grinning down at me, his eyes cold with a kind of dead weight. He looked closely at his watch. 'C'mon, follow me,' he ordered, and before I really knew what I was doing, or why, I was following him through the dimly lit camping ground, running quickly to keep up.

By the time we pulled up behind the administration block where two water tanks gave convenient cover, I was tingling with anticipation, despite the tiny voice at the back of my mind which kept speaking in the tongue of my Mum and Dad about the need for caution, for prudence, for care; of the need to stop and think and plot and plan and foresee before . . . before living.

'Wait here a minute,' Bluebeard's owner whispered, and vanished.

I could hear voices. People in the games room. Balls being pocketed. The shuffle of shoes on the raw wood floor. Conversations snatched and broken into fragments between bouts of laughter and muffled curses. The television snowing in the next room, the volume distorted, angry. And the drone of mosquitoes. They were everywhere, like the cicadas.

Idiot, I told myself. Who are you to stand around in the shadows like some macho action-fighter itching for a cause?

A door slammed and a moment later Mr Andrews appeared under the veranda. He stood tall under the fluorescent light and firmly waved the mosquitoes aside.

Nathan should be here, I told myself, not me. Nathan and Bluebeard's owner would get on, no problems.

'Come on, hurry up.'

'Where?' I managed to say, just before I was pulled through a gap in a fence.

'This way.'

I found myself under the ledge of a low, faintly lit window. The kid sat himself with his back to the weatherboard of the unit, and I had no choice but to follow.

'Smoke?' he offered as he lit his cigarette, drawing heavily and blowing the smoke away from the window.

'Listen,' I started, 'I gotta get back, you know.' The air around me was suddenly close and hot and claustrophobic. Shit, what was I doing here? I didn't even know the kid! I didn't have the slightest idea what we were doing – if we were doing anything at all.

'Sure you don't wanna smoke?' he asked. 'It'll help you relax.'

He was right; I did need calming down. I was breathing deeply, quickly, my eyes darting into the night, trying to see, to understand.

'That stuff about your name. It was just a prank. I wouldn't lose too much sleep over it.'

Easy for you to say, I thought. I shifted restlessly. Soon I would be dead. Soon, something would happen and I would be dead.

'Keep still,' Bluebeard's owner cautioned me, 'otherwise you'll scare them off.'

Them? Who was *them*?

'Look, I gotta get back,' I mouthed hopefully.

'Shuddup, willya.' Bluebeard's owner put a finger to his lips to silence me, butted out his cigarette and, getting on his knees so that he was able to peep over the window sill, tapped me on the shoulder. For a few moments I froze. Sweat washed over me. My groin ached, my teeth clamped shut.

'Listen,' Bluebeard's owner advised.

'What?'

'Shh . . . Just listen . . . Shut the fuck up and just listen.'

I did. I heard the sound of voices, indistinct and muffled.

'Look, you can see them at it.' Bluebeard's owner tapped me again and pointed through the window. 'Now that's what I call a pair of tits!'

The window was open, and though a curtain hung there it was so sheer that it might as well have been invisible. At first I couldn't see much at all in the room, but as my eyes narrowed and my ears sharpened what was going on in the room became very obvious.

I watched in open-mouthed silence. A couple were romping about naked on a large unmade bed, occasionally getting down to it. My mind cartwheeled.

'Not bad, eh,' Bluebeard's owner whispered. 'Me old man would freak if he ever found me here.' Then with a grin added, 'But not as much as me brother would if I told him

I've watched him hump Sharon maybe twenty or more times. Gee, she's got great tits. Nice arse too I reckon. What d'you think?'

I felt completely embarrassed, humiliated and ashamed. But I was also totally excited by the odd dull ache in my body; a new, blissful, sharp and excruciating sensation.

'You know what's really funny,' the kid said, not betraying a hint of how the sight might have affected him, 'Sharon knows I'm here I reckon. She has this really odd grin on her face whenever she sees me. It's kinda like a secret between us. She and me brother Chris are at it same time every day almost. Just after he gets back from work. He comes in the gates and heads straight for Sharon. Reckon if Dad's right, and rootin' before you're married makes your dick fall off, then me brother must be due for a bionic knob. He never said what happens to the girls but.' Bluebeard's owner laughed under his breath.

His dad? His *dad*?

I dropped down and fell back against the wall. 'You said Mr Andrews told you that. About the rooting and the dick business,' I said.

'Yeah, I did.'

'But just now . . .' I pointed over my head towards the room.

'Guess I never introduced meself,' Bluebeard's owner said. 'Mike . . . Mike Andrews. The Pro-prie-tor's son. At least that's what I've been told to say when I greet guests. What a wank.'

I was dumbstruck. My jeans felt horribly uncomfortable, hot and close and damp, and there was a numb ache in my belly.

'Don't look so bloody horrified, Da-vid. It's not that bad, except for havin' to look at Chris in the buff of course.' Mike Andrews produced two cigarettes, lit both and poked one into my submissive mouth where it smoked of its own accord with me hanging off its tip.

'You all right, David?' Mike Andrews asked, sucking hard on his cigarette.

When I opened my mouth the cigarette dropped out.

'Ah shit, don't waste a good smoke, mate,' Mike Andrews snapped, then added quietly, 'Look, I know it's a bit of a shock at first, but you get used to it. Once you loosen up a bit you get to enjoy what you see. You can even laugh about it.'

'I gotta go,' I muttered, eager to get away. He had no idea what he'd done to me, this kid. No idea. And not just because of what he'd taken me to perve at.

This place is your dad's, I thought, and you go around destroying property that belongs to the very people who keep the business running. If my dad had a . . .

I started crawling away, hissing back over my shoulder, 'This is sick.'

Mike Andrews flicked his cigarette butt at my back where it bounced and landed just ahead of me, 'Yeah, sure, piss off, why don'tcha. You're all the same you city kids; you don't know fuck about nothin'. You come here with a whole lotta shit in your heads about this an' that, but you're all bloody poofs and try-hards and geeks.' Then more loudly, as though he wanted the entire caravan park to hear, he added, 'I wonder whether you guys have even got a dick between your legs.'

I took off for our tent. Only when I got there did I pause long enough to look round, and there was Mike Andrews, a loose shadow merging into the night.

'Hey Wonderwog,' he called softly, 'I'll see ya next year maybe.' And then he was gone.

I waited a few moments, half expecting him to return.

When he didn't I went hastily to our tent, avoiding everyone, even Mum and her questions about why I hadn't told her where I was going, and I hopped into my sleeping bag.

'David, you okay?' she prodded. I rolled over and stared into the canvas wall.

'Yeah,' I said, 'I'm just . . . just tired.'

I wasn't a pervert, I tried consoling myself. I wasn't even particularly interested in bums and tits and stuff the way some of the guys at school seemed to be. But in the corners of my mind I knew it wasn't what I'd seen in that room that really troubled me. It was something far less tangible.

8

Back home and in my bedroom again, surrounded by all that was familiar, I wasn't sure whether the three days on Phillip Island had been worthwhile or not. Too much had happened too quickly, and none of it fitted neatly into what I'd thought my first real holiday would have been like. It wasn't just being accused of graffiti, or what Mike had shown me. It wasn't even the discovery that Mike was in fact Mr Andrews's son that really unsettled me, although I guess that had unnerved me, if only because it seemed to whisper to something deep within me about the charades that might be at work at school – with Nathan even. The fact that none of what had happened had been predictable was what had really put me on edge. Whatever, when Mum came in to fuss over what I should wear to that night's New Year's Eve dinner-dance I just wasn't in the mood to co-operate.

'Ma, I reckon I'm old enough to pick out a pair of trousers to wear, you know,' I snapped without really wanting to. Not at her, anyway.

Mum looked hurt. 'Orright ... Orright. You doan hiave to come,' she answered finally, her voice brittle. Then almost as an afterthought she added, 'I wos joust tink maibe you need haive a shirt iron.'

'I don't need a shirt ironed. I don't need my trousers picked out for me. Like I told you last year, I'd be just as happy to stay home and watch TV,' I said, knowing full well I had about as much chance of being allowed to stay home alone as Rose had of being excused from Christmas Eve Mass with 'the women.' I felt for Rose at that moment, I really did. 'I can look after myself you know. I can watch TV, read a book. I might even go to bed early . . . Anything but be bored out of my mind at the Club.'

'You doan like the Club ennimore?'

'There's nothing for me to do there.'

'Try dancing.'

'With who, *you*?'

My mother looked at me from under raised eyebrows, 'Is not so much embarrassment dance wit you mama. And if not me then wit you sister.'

Mothers, I thought! Didn't they have any memory of their own teenage years? Did *she* like dancing with her brothers? Of course it was a stupid question. I realised that the moment I'd asked it. It was stupid for two reasons: one, the village my parents came from wasn't big on dance nights, and two, my mother came from a family of poor farmers who had to rotate going to weddings amongst them because there was never enough money to afford a decent pair of shoes for all of them at once.

My mother reminded me, yet again, that I was lucky to be in a position to refuse to go to such a night. 'At your age we not hiave enough to eat, let lone tinks about go dance,' she scolded. She scouted out my best shirt, my navy pleated trousers and clean socks and then came and sat on the end of my bed. For a few moments she didn't say a word. She looked as tired as I felt, perhaps more so with all the post-holiday cleanup she was still doing.

'Maybe the holiday wasn't a good idea,' she began quietly, slipping into the comfort of her native tongue. 'Perhaps we should have stayed home. What do you think, Davide?'

'No, the holiday was a great idea,' I replied cautiously. And I meant it, despite being accused of graffitiing our tent, despite what Mike had shown me in the bedroom of the unit, despite even the confusion and discomfort I felt at that moment about – well, about everything and nothing.

'Did you enjoy yourself, Davide?' my mother was asking as I sat up. 'I mean, did you like being away from home?'

'What d'you reckon?' I answered glibly.

My mother smiled wearily. She hated it when she asked me a question in Italian and I answered in English but this time she let it pass without comment.

'I reckon mai son was enjoy his-self, but not so much so he is hiappi.'

'I'm happy, Ma. I'm just tired, okay.' I hugged her neck – a sure sign that I wasn't being totally honest – and felt her stiffen against me.

'I can see dat mai boy does not like spend time wit mother and father so much ennimore like when he was little, eh.' She laughed but it was a sad, hollow sound.

'All right, okay, I'll come,' I said too late. I could see I'd broken some spell for her.

'Your papa looks forward to his one night of the year with all his old friends,' she said, getting to her feet. 'I won't let you or Rosa – or me – spoil it for him. Do you understand me, Davide?'

I nodded.

'Do you?' she asked more forcefully. She moved slightly so that our shoulders touched and she let her gaze wander to the window that was open to the green of the park. When she spoke again her voice was low and her words measured. 'Your papa is a simple man with simple tastes. For him there are two things that are sacred. One is his belief that we – me, you, Rosa and your father – that we are Australians now that he has given his youth and every hope he ever had to this country. And the second is this family. Going to the dance is his way of showing his friends that Marco Martinesi has conquered his own ignorance and shortcomings to survive. No, not survive, prosper. He has prospered.

'When he defended you against the accusation that you had somehow been involved in the graffiti trouble at the camping ground, your father was defending his right to claim a place for us in this country, you understand. He was defending the very reasons why he came here all those years ago. Your father is a man who bruises easily. Poke him and he bruises. He cannot, will not, tolerate anyone who even suggests that he or one of his own would ever jeopardise what he came here for: a chance to better himself. And that includes being an honest and hardworking Australian. Do you understand what I'm telling you, Davide?'

We sat where we were, shoulder to shoulder, my mother staring at something only she could see beyond the window, and me too stunned by what she had said to utter anything in reply.

I wanted to tell Mum about Fernando's. I wanted to ask her what a man like my father, a man who worked two jobs, was doing in a slug-pit like that. I wanted to tell her about Mike, about the couple we'd watched. I even wanted to tell her that I knew who had written graffiti on our tent, but when I opened my mouth to speak Mum pressed her finger to my lips and told me she didn't want to hear anything that I wouldn't have told her at any other time.

I stared hard at her, bewildered.

'What I've told you stays within these four walls, Davide. Within these four walls and these four ears, understand.'

I got to my feet, put on my shoes and went ahead of her out the door. After several days confined in a space with five other people I was glad to be on my own, and more so now after my mother's well-thought-out address. She might have been trying to help me make up my mind more easily, but all she had managed to do was confuse me even more.

To avoid anyone who might be around – namely Nathan and Ralph – I took to the back streets, preferring to walk past the abandoned warehouse at the end of the street behind our house than follow the footpath to Nicholson Street and George's Fish 'n' Chip Shop.

I hungered after a piece of deep-fried, lightly salted, thinly battered flake from George's. My mother never allowed me to buy fish and chips when, as she put it, there was so much good food at home. But I had to have that piece of flake.

I wanted to believe that this little act of defiance would compensate for the torture I knew I'd have to endure that night for the sake of my father and my mother.

The quickest way to George's was to go over the fence around the warehouse, but as I picked my way through the old railway junk to one side of the boarded-up building, a sudden movement caught my eye.

I knew that kids sometimes set up headquarters here or hid out after a raid on the local shops. Nathan had often told stories about him and his mates using the warehouse to split their loot.

I knew that the warehouse was not a place my parents would want their only son to hang out. And yet I hesitated at the window, listening closely, eyes darting, breath held. It was daylight, I told myself, and from all reckoning the really nasty types probably wouldn't be inside, but I couldn't be sure.

There was a sudden burst of laughter, then sharp clapping that quickly built into a rhythm: CLAP CLAP clap clap CLAP CLAP clap clap. It sounded like the kind of signature a gang might have.

Then I heard Ralph's name – or at least the name Ralph – being called.

'R-alph . . . R-alph . . . R-alph.'

One voice started it, and others soon joined in until the name-calling and clapping became a chant: CLAP CLAP clap clap 'R-alph' CLAP CLAP clap clap 'R-alph' . . .

On and on the chant went until a second volley of laughter echoed inside. And then a new voice yelled out for silence.

The noise ceased immediately.

I froze, holding my breath. The silence seemed to last forever.

When someone finally spoke I realised that he was standing just behind the corrugated iron to my right. If I'd wanted to I could have reached around the narrow opening between it and the brickwork and touched him.

I tilted my head forward so I could peek inside the warehouse. I could see the shell of pot-holed, graffiti-smothered walls, boarded-up windows, piles and piles of rubbish, and dust veiling the air. It was a different world.

'You're a lost bloody cause, Ralph,' the voice jeered. 'You're a pathetic waste of space, a turd . . . You've got shit for brains, you retard. The only thing you're good for is to be a Welsh pup . . .' There was laughter and another round of name-calling. 'I bet you like that, you fucking mental pigmy. I bet you really get a kick – get it, a kick? – outta being

Welsh's pup.' There was a boisterous frenzy of barking, yelping and panting.

I thought I was going to piss myself, I was so scared. Not the schoolboy fear of being intimidated by the school-yard bully, or the fear of physical harm. This fear was different. It was cold and solid and sharp, and it burrowed into me, making me gasp for every breath.

The voice on the other side of the sheet of iron wasn't like any of the voices of the school-yard bullies. It had neither the teasing mockery of a Nathan Welsh, which at least assured you that you were merely a convenient target and not personally victimised, or the sarcasm used to belittle. This speaker saw Ralph as a victim; his victim, their victim.

I listened for Nathan's voice, expecting him to speak on Ralph's behalf. But it never came, and as I listened I realised that Nathan wasn't there.

My hands trembled.

'So, retard,' the voice boomed, 'with your master away you don't seem so willing to do as you're told. Not that we asked for much, did we fellas?' In the midst of the swell of agreement I heard a chair scrape and feet shuffle but I didn't flinch, didn't dare try to look inside.

'It's not as though we asked you to do the impossible. All you had to do was get into the place through the back window, check it out for us, then let us in through the back door. I reckon even a shithead like you, you bastard Welsh puppy dog, even you couldn't fuck that up. But you did. What I'd like to know now, Ralph, is why you let us down. I mean, it's not as though that bastard Gaglieri pays you a fortune to work for him. He makes a packet don't you know, a packet. He's got you working for peanuts while he makes enough money to buy himself a new fucking car every year, and you – you, you stupid retard – you don't even get why you should help us break in . . .

'And not only that, but you embarrass me in front of me mates. Me, your one true brother in the whole fucking world. Me, who steps in to stop Dad knocking your retard head off your shoulders. Me, who had to cop all the slack because you're too much of a shit-brain to know that Dad don't like to be woken up after he's been on the piss all bloody night . . . You're a loser Ralph, a real dead-set waste of skin and bones. I can't even fucking believe we're related. Let's face it Ralph, you're a bloody embarrassment to the human race.'

Again there was laughter, malevolent and threatening, like thunder.

'Ralph ain't an embarrassment to the human race – he's more vegetable than human,' yelled another voice. The others clapped in approval.

I blinked hard, hard enough to hurt my eyes. I couldn't believe what I was hearing. It wasn't possible, I told myself. I'd either heard wrong or else – or else this voice that I was hearing was the most callous, most loathsome voice I'd ever heard.

And what was Ralph doing? Why had they been chanting his name? Why didn't he answer his brother? Surely, surely if nothing else, Ralph could reason with his brother? But about what, I wondered. About not having broken into his workplace? About being called all those names?

But what I did know? What I felt as a tingle down my spine was that I had overheard something not meant for my ears. To even repeat to myself what I'd heard, especially about the intended break-in, was to offer myself as a sacrifice to these thugs.

I was no hero, I reminded myself. Why should I tell

anyone what I'd overheard? What could I do to help if Ralph's brother and his mates decided to beat him up – if they hadn't already.

I swallowed, knowing that there was nothing I could do. I was 'Dottore', the intellectual one. Fat lot of good it did me now, I told myself, and hated myself for it. Nathan would have done something; he'd have known what to do, but not me. What could I do?

I could get my dad, sure. He'd know what to do. I could call for my mum even. She was always ready to protect. I could run for Zio Paul. He'd know what to do. He'd roughed it.

Go for the leader. That was the trick. I'd heard about that tactic at school. I'd heard my Zio Paul talk about it too. Take out the leader and chances are you scare off the gang, cutting its head as it were, that's what he'd said. Go for the leader. Cut off the monster's head. Go for the top gun . . . Yeah, that's what I had to do, should do . . .

Where was Nathan? He should have been there. He *should* have been there.

I was just too scared.

And so I waited, rooted to the spot, uncertain of my ability to fight, afraid of being hurt, until finally the voices inside the warehouse died to a murmur. The silence that followed was deep and painful. I could hear my heart pounding in my throat. Pounding with fear. With disgust.

Suddenly there was a screech of iron and Ralph tumbled out of a window at my back. There was no time to duck behind anything. Miraculously, nobody saw me, and they quickly pulled the sheet of iron back into place.

'Run home little puppy, run home,' someone called.

I dropped to the ground and watched Ralph where he lay in a heap. I kept hidden.

If only Nathan were here, I found myself thinking again, and immediately I was ashamed of myself. But not so ashamed that I could step out from my hiding place and help Ralph to his feet, nor help him brush down his clothes or wipe his lip where it bled. Nor ashamed enough to follow Ralph when he stumbled towards the fence, crying.

The minute Ralph was over the fence and out of sight I ran in the opposite direction, sick to the stomach. I felt as if I had been the one who had been taunted.

I ran and I ran, until I was right out of breath and gulping for air.

9

That night I couldn't get Ralph and what I'd stumbled upon out of my mind. As always I didn't dance, but that was no big deal. Rose noticed the off-hand way I kept dismissing any of the guys who came up to talk to me though.

'So, Big Brother, too good for the old crowd, hey?' she said without a hint of surprise. 'This time next year and, who knows, you too could be a shining role model for the less blessed of the world.'

'Take a hike, Rose,' I snarled. She backed away. 'Don't get all aggro with me, David Martinesi. You're the one acting like someone's put a broomstick up your arse. "Sorry guys, I don't feel like talking. Sorry guys, I don't want to go outside and check out Aldo's new wheels. Sorry guys ..."'

'I'm warning you, Rose. Back off.'

But Rose wouldn't. '"Can't have a game of soccer out in the foyer boys, we're not kids any more, you know guys. Grow up why don'tchas ..."'

'SHUT THE FUCK UP, ROSE!' I bellowed so that the entire table turned to look at me, and my father, who was up the other end having a beer, gave me the evil eye: You're dead!

'Just shut up, Rose. Okay? Please.'

Rose shut up and pressed herself deeper into the vinyl chair.

'I hate this place,' she said after a few minutes, ripping at the paper tablecloth with the tips of her nails. 'I'm on your side. This place is a bore. I'd rather be knitting bed socks with Nonna than in this shit heap.'

She was quiet a while longer, then, leaning into me she whispered, 'If I told you I've decided to go steady, would you dob on me?'

I looked at her. Rose, going steady? She was just a kid!

'It's a bit of a useless question isn't it, given that you've told me anyway.' I grinned back. 'If Dad finds out he'll chain you to your bedroom wall and have you hand fed until it's time for you to find a husband. Or rather, until they've found one for you.'

'He wouldn't. You don't know him the way I do. And besides, he won't know because no one's going to tell him, are they?'

The dance floor was crowded. Young and old couples alike were doing their best not to get tangled up together. It was close to midnight and the Social Committee was preparing for the countdown by arranging a huge clock near the stage and dressing one of their members as Old Father time, another as New Father Time.

'Who's the lucky boy then?' I asked, not really convinced there was anyone. After all, Rose was almost two years younger than I was *and* she was a Martinesi girl.

'Wouldn't you like to know,' Rose shot back through a laugh.

'Stuff you, Rose. Go play with the other munchkins why don'tcha.'

Rose tore a long strip from the tablecloth then folded it

and folded it again until she had a tiny square in the palm of her hand. 'His name's Chris, and he's Toula's cousin.'

'A Greek!' My voice was more strident than I'd intended and again everyone looked at me. I lowered my tone. 'A Greek. Are you out of your fucking mind, Rose? Having a boyfriend is one way to get onto death row, but a Greek boyfriend ... Rose, I think you got too much sun on the island, you know what I mean?'

Rose shook her head slowly. 'You surprise me, David Angelo Martinesi. You really surprise me. For all your put-on about Mum and Dad being too particular about who we hang out with, you're just as narrow-minded as they are.'

'He's a Greek, Rose,' I said, trying to make her see the dilemma she was putting herself into. 'Mum and Dad have a hard enough time trying to imagine that one day you might come home and announce you've decided you want to go out with a guy. But someone who doesn't even speak the lingo ... Rose, please. Why don't you just go step in front of a bus? Or better still, why don't you waltz over to Dad right now and tell him his future son-in-law is a Greek.'

I hadn't meant to laugh. What Rose had told me wasn't amusing at all. I tried to win back some ground. 'Look Rose, I'm sorry. I've got nothing against Greeks. In fact, I reckon George down at the fish shop is one of the best blokes around, but ... Rose, you've got to look at it from Mum and Dad's point of view. How will it look if their daughter brings home someone they can't even have a decent conversation with?'

For a moment Rose didn't say a word, concentrating on the tips of her fingers as she pressed them together. When she did speak her voice was brittle.

'You can spend your life looking at things from Mum and

Dad's point of view if you like, David,' she said. 'You can even pretend to yourself that you like it, that their way is the only way of looking at the world. Just don't be surprised if the rest of us move on, okay?'

The rest of the night was pretty uneventful. The band stuffed up their usual quota of songs. The club's president bored us shitless with a speech about how we should all support his niece as the club's entrant in the Miss Italo-Australia Quest. And Dad got just drunk enough to try and fondle Mum in front of us. At some stage I must have gone into a state of suspended animation and finally deep sleep because it was morning again before I realised we'd made it home intact. When I looked up, Rose was standing in her nightgown in my doorway staring at me.

'David?' she whispered.

'WHAT?' I snapped.

'Da-vid,' she repeated, and this time I caught the lilt in her voice.

'Listen Rose, I'm really stuffed, so if ...' I didn't get to finish my sentence before Rose walked into the room and stood at the foot of my bed. 'Shit Rose, what's wrong?' I struggled to sit up, trying to focus, 'Why're you crying? Don't tell me ... it's Dad, right? He's found out about Chris the Greek. Oh fuck, Rose, you're in deep shit now.'

Rose shook her head, 'Something terrible's happened ... it's ... Zio Paul. He's ...'

'What are you on about Rose?'

Rose was trembling now and swallowing air as though it were water. 'Nonna, Zio Sandro and Zio Paul had a huge fight last night ... when Zio Sandro went to pick Nonna up ... and ... and ... and ...' She burst out crying again and ran from the room. I followed her into the kitchen where I found Mum and Dad huddled around Nonna, who was crumpled in a chair.

Nonna didn't look up when I entered, and for a moment I thought she might have been dead she was so hunched over, so folded in on herself. As I drew closer she wailed loudly. I jumped and stepped sideways into Dad, who lowered his eyes and put a finger to his lips. Mum motioned for Rose and me to leave the room. She might even have pushed Rose and me out physically had Nonna not gone into a fit of hysterics that demanded her attention.

It was left to Dad to usher us into the hallway and back to the bedroom. 'Stay here and keep quiet,' he said softly but firmly, as he shut the door on us.

'What's going on, Rose?' I asked.

Rose caught her breath, 'Zio Paul and Zio Sandro had a big fight.'

'So? They're always at each other, that's no drama.'

'It is when Zio Sandro thinks his brother has disgraced the family by bringing a girlfriend round to meet Nonna unannounced.' Rose plonked herself on the end of my bed and rubbed her eyes. 'She's Australian. She's some woman none of us has ever heard of – not that that would make much difference to Machiavelli.'

I'd never heard Rose refer to Zio Sandro by that name before, and I grinned despite myself. 'So he's brought this woman home. He's done that before, too. I don't see – '

'He told Nonna this woman was his girlfriend and that he was taking her to Zio Sandro's with them for dinner.'

'Without warning Zia Graziella or getting the permission slip in triplicate from Machiavelli? He must be out of his mind.' I had been trying to lighten the mood but I didn't succeed. Rose told me to grow up and stop being so selfish.

'Selfish? Yeah, good one, Rose. And how do you work that out?'

Rose took a long breath and then fixed me with her eyes the way Mum did when she was angry with me. 'David Martinesi, you're a real worry. You talk shit because you know shit. Maybe if you paid a little more attention to the crap that flies around this family whenever someone dares to do something no one approves of, you'd see why Zio Paul probably had no choice.'

'And you do, Missy, do you?' I hissed back. 'You've really got a handle on how this family operates, have you? That's why you've gone and got yourself a fucking Greek for a boyfriend!'

Suddenly Rose was on her feet, tears running down her face. 'Maybe. And maybe Zio Paul did what he did because he knows *exactly* how this family "operates", as you put it.'

I turned away from Rose, listening to the wave of jumbled voices that washed in from the kitchen as she left my room.

I finally worked up the courage to go and stand next to Rose behind the kitchen door in the hallway.

'It's God's punishment to me for moving my family from their real home,' Nonna kept repeating. 'It serves me right. I deserve to be punished.' With surprising calm Mum replied, 'Everyone is being ridiculous about this. Zio Paul is a grown man and grown men do not run away simply because their brother has offended them.'

Zio Sandro suggested the family was probably better off without 'that big child'.

'If anyone has acted like a big child,' countered Mum, 'it is Zio Sandro.'

Why wasn't Mum fretting over Zio Paul the way Nonna had been? I suspected that Mum knew more than she was letting on. But at that moment she wasn't about to betray her confidence to anyone, no matter how often Nonna threatened suicide or Zio Sandro suggested alerting the police to track down Zio Paul as though he were a naughty boy. What Mum did do, however, when Nonna had finally exhausted herself into a restless sleep and Zio Sandro had decided no one was on his side and had gone off home in a huff, was to huddle Rose and me into my bedroom, and tell us why we had to keep to ourselves all that we'd seen and heard.

'People talk,' she said flatly. 'Especially when they don't know the whole story. They invent as they go. Give your neighbours a hint of gossip and watch them build an entire scandal around it.

'Zio Paul has done something stupid, but not unexpected,' she added hesitantly. 'He's got a hard head sometimes and won't listen to reason.'

'It's because she's Australian that Zio Sandro reacted the way he did, isn't it?' Rose asked.

'That, and because Zio Sandro thinks he can have a say in our lives because he's the eldest male.' Mum spoke without smiling. She was a long time between words. 'When Nonno died, Zio Sandro became head of the house, and as such he believes he has a right to comment on how Zio Paul and I live, what we do with our lives.'

'You too, Ma?' Rose asked genuinely surprised. 'How?'

Mum stroked Rose's cheek, her eyes locked on mine. She could see that, unlike Rose, I wasn't at all surprised. 'In many ways, but not any more,' she answered without real conviction. 'Not like he used to.'

As Mum spoke, I wasn't surprised to learn that Zio Sandro had tried to stop her from marrying Dad. Zio Sandro and Dad went back a long way it turned out; they had both courted the girl who became my Zia Graziella. Zio Sandro had asked spies amongst the small community of *paesani* in Melbourne to report back to him on Mum's every move. And Machiavelli had taken to writing to Mum in Nonna's name begging her to ignore Marco Martinesi's advances. Zio Sandro wasn't going to let an old rival just waltz in and marry *his* sister.

'Oh God,' sobbed Rose when Mum had finished, 'Zio Paul's really run away this time.'

10

The New Year's Day festivities were put on hold while everyone – except Zio Sandro and his family – tried to sort out the confusion. Zio Graziella claimed they had prior arrangements that couldn't be altered.

After Dad and Mr Valdo had exhausted all avenues of inquiry and Nonna had been reassured that her son had not become the victim of an evil enchantress, Mum called me aside and asked whether I could be trusted to run an important errand with her. I thought she was being melo-dramatic, but I soon discovered that whatever it was she wanted me to help her do was of great importance to her.

'My son and I have to go out,' she told Dad more firmly than I ever thought she would have dared.

My father looked up from where he sat at the table with Mr Valdo.

'Rose, you help Nonna get your father and Pietro something to eat,' Mum went on. When Rose made as though to protest Mum raised a hand, and whatever Rose wanted to say evaporated.

'You and your son, you can't wait until later, until after we've eaten,' my father said with a half-hearted scowl. 'This whatever it is you have to do, it can't wait?'

'It's already waited too long,' my mother said as she left the room.

I started to follow but my father pulled me over towards the kitchen window, where we stood for a moment looking out at the park. He was wearing the shirt Rose and I had given him for his birthday. It was a little tight around the neck, and his chin seemed to gather in a thick knot behind the top button. Sixty years old, I thought suddenly, and wished he'd had me a few years before he did. I wished that with all my heart.

'Your mother,' he said, and slipped a ten dollar note into my hand. 'She . . . she sometimes forgets that not everyone wants her advice. But I want you to promise me you won't let her down today. Listen when she talks to you.' He lowered his voice and narrowed his eyes. 'Don't be like your Zio Paul, Davide. Sometimes a word from a woman with heart can be a salvation. You understand?'

I didn't, and to cover my awkwardness I said, 'I don't need any money, Dad.'

'Keep it anyway, David,' he replied in English. 'I not want you go out with you mother and not be able even buy her a coffee.' He laughed under his breath but the smile never crossed his face and he turned back into the room.

Mum and I didn't speak all the long walk to the tram stop out the front of George's Fish 'n' Chip Shop, where a hand-scrawled sign read: No bisniss todai.

We waited a while for a tram but Mum was in no mood to hang around, so she hailed a cab. We were dropped off near St Vincents Hospital.

'Where are we going?' I asked for the first time. My spine tingled.

'Come with me,' Mum said by way of reply, and she led me down a narrow cobbled laneway.

We followed the high iron fence along and stopped at a door marked 12A. When my mother reached up to unlatch it, I could tell that this place was familiar to her. That startled me.

When we were inside the messy back yard Mum turned and spoke to me. Her voice was steady. 'You wait here for me. I won't be very long. I don't want you to worry or to call out. I just want you to wait here until I come back.'

'Why?' I protested. 'What's going on?' There was no way I wanted her to go anywhere on her own, and no way I was going to stand there surrounded by decades of junk and filth without at least an explanation.

When my mother put her finger to her lips for silence I refused to oblige. 'No,' I said, 'I'm sick of being kept in the dark about what goes on in this family . . . I've got as much right as – '

Mum grabbed my arm and glared at me. 'You are not to say one word, Davide,' she said through gritted teeth. 'Not *one* word, do you understand?'

I nodded feebly, but I didn't really understand at all. Nothing was really understandable any more, it seemed, nothing.

When Mum knocked on the door I felt something shift in my belly.

We waited in silence, my mum and me, for what seemed like ages. I looked about me. A broken armchair was home to a mangy ginger and grey cat. Around the chair plastic pots held shrivelled azaleas, a sprig or two of rosemary, a wilted camellia, and the frayed ends of what could have been a tomato plant. Against the wall, by the door, was a table, one leg a tower of bricks. And balanced on the table, all splattered with green paint, were piles of newspapers, dried-out paint brushes and a battered pair of men's boots.

I blinked, stupefied. My skin crawled and in my throat a dry lump rose and fell. It almost exploded when there was a sound of movement behind the door and a voice, a woman's voice, called to ask us to identify ourselves.

'Is Teresa here,' my mum answered. 'Is sister of Paul, me.'

The door opened a fraction and one eye appeared in the gap before what my mother had said fully registered.

'You me need talk,' my mother said bluntly.

At first the woman at the gap seemed not to have heard. Her eye trained on me a few moments then a second later she held the door open wide enough for us to enter. Or so I thought.

'*Aspetta qua*,' Mum ordered. 'I not be long.' And before I could complain the door closed firmly in my face.

'Ma?' I called, but the door remained shut.

This couldn't be where Zio Paul was, I told myself. No way. But that woman, whoever she was – perhaps even the woman my uncle had bolted out of Nonna's house with – she seemed to recognise my mum. 'Is Teresa here,' Mum had said, 'Is sister of Paul.' But that didn't make any sense at all. I knew all my mother's friends and acquaintances; like the woman at the door, they were all about her age, but I couldn't remember ever having seen *this* woman.

No, this couldn't be the woman Machiavelli had rejected the night before. She was much too old for Zio Paul. Zio Paul was young, a kid by comparison.

I was cold to the bone. Too much, I told myself. Too much too soon. Nathan. Ralph. The holiday. Mike ... And now this! God, the confusion . . .

And to top it all off, I knew absolutely nothing about this woman Mum had come to see, or this house with its stench of cat piss and damp. For all I knew the woman who had come to the door might be none too keen to see Mum – and then what?

Was Zio Paul inside too? Was that it? Was Mum inside reasoning with Zio Paul? If so, why hadn't he come out to say hello? If not, why was Mum taking so long?

'Is my uncle in there?' I asked the cat. I growled at it and it hissed back. 'I bet Mum's in there right now, telling that woman to let Zio go, to leave him alone. It *is* her isn't it – the woman Zio Paul brought home to Nonna?' The cat looked back at me, unblinking. I threw a paint brush at it, and it shrieked and slunk away.

I tried to peer in the window, but the curtains were too heavy, and besides, there must have been a few year's worth of grime on the glass.

I was about to try the door when it suddenly swung open. If my mother hadn't grabbed me I would have fallen and taken the woman at her side down with me.

'*Andiamo*. We go now,' Mum said as she helped me right myself.

There was nothing I could do to hide my embarrassment so I avoided meeting their eyes, glancing instead into the dimness of the house. And that's when I saw Zio Paul.

He was slumped in a chair, leaning forward, his hands clutching his head, elbows on his knees, as though he were in enormous pain.

'Ma?' I heard myself whimper from somewhere deep down inside, and then the door swung to.

Mum and I didn't catch a taxi home; we walked instead.

The streets of Fitzroy were largely deserted, with the exception of a few homeless people who wandered about Gertrude Street and around the Carlton Gardens.

Mum kept us to the opposite side of the road when we passed the boarding houses that rang with too-loud music and the drone of static from radios perched on wicker chairs under crumbling awnings. She hadn't held my hand in years, but now she clutched my right one tightly, walking heavily, pounding the footpath.

'Did you talk to him, Ma? Is he coming home? What will you tell Nonna?' I asked once the gold statue of the Blessed Virgin was clearly visible ahead of us atop the bell tower of Our Lady Help of Christians Church.

Not far away, the silos loomed as large as ever, and Mum suddenly stopped and faced me.

'I want you to promise me something, Davide,' she whispered, dropping my hand and slipping her arm through mine. 'I want you to promise me that no matter who you may marry, or who Rosa might one day marry, promise me that you will never turn against your sister, Davide. Promise me, that for the sake of your sister you will swallow your own pride and always be ready to side with her.' She tugged lightly on my arm so that I faced her properly. 'Promise me, Davide,' she repeated.

'I promise,' I whispered without thought, my father's words echoing now in my mind. Listen to her. Listen to her . . .

Mum smiled thinly. I wondered what this had to do with Nonna or Zio Paul.

'Davide,' Mum went on, her Italian crisp, 'some time ago your Zio Paolo came to see me about this woman friend of his. We communicate in a certain way, your Zio and I. My God, we have had to fight against the same forces all our lives, especially since Papa died.' She grinned sadly, 'Well, let's say that your Zio Sandro can be a very hard man. Hard of head. Hard of heart. But that's not all his fault. It's not easy to be the eldest in a family whose breadwinner dies, leaving you to pick up the pieces. Anyway, your Zio Paolo came to see me – and your father – about Joan, and he told us all about her three children, her vagrant ex-husband . . . and the fact that he wanted to move out of Nonna's home and go and live with her.

'Your Zio Paolo found this bungalow for Joan and her children after the ex-husband came looking for them.' My mother stabbed the air. 'I told him that I had nothing against Joan. How could I? I had never met her. But I told him too, that there are never such things as ex-husbands or ex-wives, not where there are children concerned. Your Zio mistook commonsense for betrayal and stormed out.'

She paused. 'He came back though. He came again and again, each time opening up that little boy heart of his to your father and me.' She turned and looked at me for a long moment, then said calmly, 'Paolo left school at the same age as you are now, Davide. Rather than get a job or an apprenticeship he moved out of home and into a flat with his friends . . . From that moment the animosity between my two brothers grew worse and worse . . . Sandro even went after Paolo, having decided he would drag him back to Nonna's by the hair if he had to . . .

'You couldn't know of course, and I'm trembling even now as I tell you this, but Paolo's friends beat your Zio Sandro until he could barely stand. They hit him and hit him until he was like a rag at their feet. And then they fled. The three of them . . . your Zio Paolo included.'

I felt my mother's hand close tightly around mine. She covered her mouth with her other hand and stared directly ahead. I hesitated. 'Did Zio Paul . . . Did he . . .'

'Beat up his own brother? No, but he was too scared, too disoriented . . . too . . . I don't know what, to stop the others. So of course he ran off with them. He ran off and we didn't hear from him for three years. Three long, black years. And in that time your Zio Sandro swore that he would never allow Paolo to set foot in his or Nonna's house again. He felt cheated, robbed, after having done all he could to put Paolo and me on the right path. Too bad if we didn't agree that his path was the right one.

'Your Zio Sandro has had a hard life too,' Mum explained. Her voice was soft, empty of any malice. 'Nothing has been easy for him either. From the moment our father died Sandro became the man of the house. It was his burden to make certain Paolo and I were set on "the right path". But where I have always been quite compliant, your Zio Paolo has had a head of his own. He never liked his brother meddling in his life. Never. Not from the moment Sandro stepped into our father's shoes.'

This was all news to me and Mum knew it. She kept right on talking though, right over my babbling.

Yes, my Zio Paolo had been in trouble with the police as a much younger man, she told me, without a hint of judgement. Petty things mainly: street fights, car theft, no drugs or anything like that.

'Your Zio Paolo was, and is, easily influenced,' Mum was quick to point out. Basically he was an honest and good person. Yet no matter how much he had tried not to, Zio Paolo had drifted back time and time again to the ways of his friends.

I wanted Mum to stop talking, to pause and let what she was telling me sink in. My legs struggled to keep up with her pace.

'It was your father who finally tracked Paolo down,' my

mother continued as we turned the corner of our street. 'For three years your Zio lived off his wits and God knows how else. When your father found him Paolo had only recently returned to Melbourne and had decided – for his own reasons – that maybe it was time to return home. Our Italian community was a lot closer back then than it is now, and your Zio put out word as to where he could be found.'

For the first time since she had started speaking my mother smiled. 'At first Sandro wanted to go and fetch Paolo, but we talked him out of it since most probably he would have killed Paolo. It was decided your father would go and find him instead.'

We stopped suddenly. We were only about a block from home. I was suffocatingly hot, my clothes pasted to my skin. But not from the heat.

I expected to see tears in Mum's eyes, but her eyes were dark and still and frighteningly cold.

'My brother Paolo is not a bad man,' she said in a voice just above a whisper. 'He grew up without a father, went to school in a country that made fun of his ignorance and culture, and got lost. My brother is a little boy lost. Lost from himself, from Zio Sandro, from Nonna. And after today, maybe from me too.'

She paused long enough to take a breath.

'How did I know where to find him today? I'll tell you,' she continued, and began walking again, more slowly than before. 'My brother Paolo and I have always been close, especially after your Zio Sandro came out here and did his best to make my life with your father hell. Paolo was always there to stand up for me, to calm your father down. He has a special fondness for your papa, Davide, because your father became the father he'd lost, and the older brother he'd lost to sheer pride and stubbornness.

'Your Zio Paolo told us about Joan, about how he'd met her, what he felt for her, months ago. He wanted to bring her home to introduce her to Nonna and he came to see your Papa and me for advice. I told him I wanted to meet Joan, and he agreed.'

My mother tossed her head back slightly and I saw the rugged lines etched into her neck. I swallowed hard to clear the lump in my throat.

'She's a nice lady, much older than Paolo of course. We talked when we met at the bungalow, and I told her – and my brother – not to rush, not to startle Nonna or Zio Sandro. They are people with little room for change, your Zio Sandro and Nonna. I told Paolo and Joan to wait until I felt I could talk to Nonna, break the news to her, explain to her that her little boy had grown up, that he would be all right on his own. I wanted to talk to Zio Sandro too.'

'And Zio Paul didn't wait.'

Mum shook her head. 'No, he didn't wait. He'd already waited a lifetime,' she said. 'He wasn't prepared to wait any longer for his brother and mother to accept his decisions.'

Dad was waiting by the gate as we approached. He looked at me and grinned nervously, his face less harsh than it had been that morning.

Mum didn't say a word as she went ahead of me indoors. When I looked at my father he simply raised his eyebrows, the way he sometimes does when something important has passed between himself and someone else. Only now I sensed that the someone else was me.

That night in bed I thought again about what my Zio had said about how if only he'd had more friends like me when he was growing up, he might have made more of himself.

I had never known that side of him, running away as a teenager, trouble with the law, getting into the wrong crowd. This all made sense of everything Zio Paul had said to me on Christmas Day as we'd sat in the back yard trying to confide in each other.

For the first time in my life I felt that perhaps I might not be confined to a bleak and predictable future as a stay-at-home. Perhaps my Uncle Paul had been right. Perhaps Nathan Welsh was just looking for someone different from all the other friends he had. I was certainly that.

What wasn't so clear, though, was why me? Why of all the nerdy, piss-weak stay-at-homes had Nathan Welsh singled me out?

11

'You may not be a stay-at-home any more, Martinesi, but you're sure as shit a fair dinkum wog,' was how Nathan greeted me the first time we saw each other after I got back from Phillip Island.

Not that I can blame him, for right at that moment I was soaping down the venetian blinds Mum had hung on a length of rope stretched between our garage and the fence.

'Yeah, well, you know what it's like,' I answered. 'We wogs wash and disinfect our houses, you Skips rinse out your plates with beer and hose down your clothes once every so often ... It's tradition I guess. A blood thing.'

'At least that's the only piss we drink,' Nathan snorted back, but there was no anger in his voice. 'You guys go ape-shit over fermented grape juice.'

'Don't forget the snags, mate,' I reminded him, hosing the blinds down quickly.

There was heaps I wanted to tell Nathan about my holiday. Well, perhaps not heaps. I could skip the part about the mussel hunt, for instance. And getting lost on the way to the island. But the bit about the naked couple would be worth a few points in my favour. And the bit about Mr Andrews yelling at me for swearing outside the games room.

It was funny. A few short weeks ago there would have been no way I'd have told Nathan Welsh anything about my life. Yet now I'd even decided to tell him about Zio Paul. I sensed that just as Zio Paul had understood when I'd confided in him about Nathan, so too would Nathan understand when I told him about Zio Paul – and how devastated I felt about his sudden disappearance from my life.

'What about the snags?' Nathan pulled himself up into a sitting position on the fence. Instinctively I looked over my shoulder. Rose was by the back door but she didn't seem too interested in us.

'We Italians use real pig's meat to make ours. I'm told you Skips whack in a bit of sawdust, a handful of pencil shavings, that kind of thing . . .' It felt okay to joke with Nathan like this.

He yawned expansively. 'So, how was the great adventure?' he asked.

I didn't answer immediately, trailing the stream of water from the hose in an arc over the blinds. No matter how comfortable I was beginning to feel around Nathan, we weren't so far beyond mutual distrust and suspicion that I could abandon all caution.

'He-llo . . .' Nathan called. 'He-llo, anyone h-o-o-me?'

'I saw a couple, you know, doing it,' I said suddenly. 'This guy Mike took me to see them. She wasn't bad – big tits, nice arse. She wasn't exactly hot, but she was okay, you know.'

I half expected Nathan to laugh, or at least to interrupt me. When he did neither I told him what I'd seen, embellishing it a bit. Mike and I were crouched not under a window sill but behind the wardrobe in the same room; the woman didn't just moan with pleasure, she screamed and squealed; the man didn't merely kiss the woman, he licked and bit her.

Nathan listened without comment. When I'd finished he scratched the side of his head, blinked hard, then asked, 'Did you come in your jocks?'

'Nah,' I replied. 'Unlike some people, I can control myself. I don't have a problem with premature evacuation – eja – I mean . . .' It was too late; the word had slipped out.

'Shit,' I spat as I shook my head in anger against Nathan's laughter. To deflect my embarrassment I asked, 'So why didn't you show?'

I saw Nathan shift his weight uncomfortably on the fence. It was only a momentary action, the putting of all his weight on both wrists as he flexed his back. But I saw something ripple across Nathan's face, something that I knew wasn't meant to be seen.

'How long you gonna be with that?' he asked, looking past me.

'Done,' I replied, 'but you still haven't answered my question. How come you didn't show up at Phillip Island like you threatened you would?'

'I was busy.'

'I knew you wouldn't come,' I lied. Nathan was dodging the subject. I tried a different approach. 'You just said what you did to shit me. You knew you weren't going anywhere near the island, you just – '

'Quit it!' Nathan's voice stung the air. He was looking straight at me again, unblinking. 'Just drop it, okay. You aren't so long from being a mere stay-at-home that a few words from me in the right places couldn't cancel it all for you . . .'

I didn't pursue the topic.

'How long your folks been married, Martinesi?' Nathan asked suddenly.

I told him that I was born just short of ten months after their wedding night and that if I'd been born premature Nonna would have taken out a contract on Dad.

'You Italians really get into this having-kids stuff quick-smart like,' Nathan observed. 'My folks waited seven years to have me, and even then they fucked it up – if you get my drift.'

I didn't.

'The seven year itch,' Nathan said, lighting a cheap cigar. 'My old man got the itch between his legs the day after I was born and hit the bitumen, shot through . . .'

'Oh,' I said.

'Yeah, oh, all right,' Nathan sneered. He drew heavily on the cigar, tossed his head back and looked away into the cloudless sky. 'Mum reckons the old man hung around long enough to take the pats on the back and the free handouts of – ' He looked at the cigar in his hand and held it up, 'these, then he left.

'So, you want to know why I didn't show at Phillip Island Mr Perfect Family Man? My mum's latest boyfriend decided to *surprise* us both with a last-minute change of plan. "Let's do something different. You can go to the island any time," he told my mum the morning we left when we were already on the road. "The old shack'll still be there next year," he said. "It won't blow away." And he drove us to Wodonga instead.

'You with me, Martinesi? This dumb arse-hole decided upon the spur of the moment that he didn't want to spend two weeks with me and Mum in the shack Nan and Pops had rented. No, bloody Tim wanted to be alone with us. "A family" he called us, the prick.

'I would've tracked you down too, Martinesi, sooner or later. I would've found you no worries.' Nathan spoke quickly, as though struggling to get the words out. 'I wasn't talking shit at school, Martinesi, don't you go daydreaming about that. And I would've hitchhiked to the island too, but for Mum. Mum didn't seem to mind not going to her folks. She even laughed like a bloody schoolgirl who's just seen her first dick when she phoned Nan to tell her the news.

'"We're going to Wodonga, Mum," she said. "Me, Tim and Nathan, the three of us." Musketeers, she called us. I could've throttled her, I swear. When she didn't insist we go to Phillip Island, I wanted to strangle her, I was so pissed off. Not about the island, as much as . . . as much as . . .'

Nathan never finished his sentence. I was shocked by what he'd said, and by the fact that he'd actually said it – and to me of all people.

Nathan took a small pouch from his pocket and held it out to me.

'What's that?' I asked, without taking my eyes off him.

'It's a present. Go on, take it.' I took the pouch and he added, 'So, tell us, what d'you think of Ralph?'

I'd been expecting this question ever since first meeting Ralph. But now that it had been asked I wasn't sure what to say – especially after the scene at the warehouse. I picked at the pouch. My hesitation was long enough to oblige Nathan to fill the awkward silence.

'Most people find Ralph a nuisance. He tends to get in the way a lot, as though he's got no control over his body. He's seventeen, but if you'd only ever heard him talk and not actually got a look at him, you'd have to swear he was probably about ten years old. He's big and strong and clumsy. He's got no footy skills, can't bounce a ball to save his life. He runs like a pregnant wombat, and he couldn't hit the side of the silos with a demolition ball even if he was standing nose up against the thing.'

Nathan watched me poking about in the pouch. I saw him out of the corners of my eyes and tried a smile.

'You talk to Ralph sometimes, most times, you're like, talking to yourself. He hears you fine, but you kinda doubt that the receivers are turned on. So you keep talking and talking until you feel like a frigging nut-case, so you go shoot pool, smoke the joint he's pinched off his dickhead brother, or just fool around.'

I'd stopped trying to find anything in the pouch. It was empty. Sucked in again, Martinesi!

Nathan noticed I'd clenched my fist around the pouch, and he held out his hand for it. That's when I swallowed hard and pushed the question out of my mouth. 'Why did you tell me about what happened with your dad, and about . . . about . . .'

'Tim?' Nathan finished off for me. He chewed the cigar end roughly and spat out of the corner of his mouth.

'Same reason you took this,' he said, holding up the empty pouch.

'Because you gave it to me,' I said stiffly, starting to feel as though I'd been set up.

'You took this from me,' Nathan went on slowly, 'because you trusted me. You wouldn't have taken the pouch if you thought it was empty, would you? No. You trusted me enough to believe there was something in it for you, right? Well, I guess I've told you some things, shown you some things I haven't told or shown anyone else because I trust you, Martinesi.'

With that he took something from his pocket. I couldn't see what it was because he seemed to have purposely concealed it in his fist. He watched me closely, and then opened his fist. In his outstretched palm was a small key.

'Lose this key, Martinesi, and one day I'll come back and hunt you down for keeps.' He said it with a smile but I shuddered nonetheless. 'I'll hunt you down, David Martinesi. Lose this and I'll hunt you down for keeps.'

'What's it for?' I eventually asked, turning the key over in my hand.

'It's a key, Martinesi. It unlocks things. Doors . . . Locks.'

'And you want me to have it? W-why?'

Nathan took a deep breath and cocked his head back, looking hard at me. 'Because I trust you, Martinesi,' he said. 'I trust you not to go blab at school about Ralph. I trust you not to go shooting your mouth off at school or anywhere else about what I've just told you. And I trust you to look after – '

'What, Nathan? Look after what?'

But Nathan wouldn't say.

'So, you still haven't answered my question,' he said instead. 'What do you think of our mate Ralph?'

I wondered whether I should tell him about what had gone on at the warehouse. And as to what I thought about Ralph, I couldn't say exactly. I sensed Ralph needed friends, wanted friends – yet I wasn't sure I was the type of person who could be the sort of friend Ralph needed. After all, I had done nothing to help him at the warehouse.

'My uncle has run away from home,' I announced as we walked. 'He had a blue with his brother and my Nonna over a woman and he just pissed off.' When Nathan didn't respond I pressed ahead. 'He has this girl-friend who's – '

'She's not Italian, right,' Nathan finished for me.

I narrowed my eyes, 'Yeah. How'd you know?'

'What else do Italian boys run away from home over,' he

laughed back. 'It's so bloody obvious isn't it? You Italians – but not just you Italians – the lot of you.'

'Ethnics?'

'A lot of you migrants, you want everything Australia can offer: work, money, a place of your own . . . stuff like that. But you wanna keep to yourselves at the same time. You wanna be Australians but only in a material sense. All hell breaks out if one of you wants to crossbreed. Shit, the Mafris went nuts when one of Mr Mafri's sisters told the family she was gonna marry a guy from England. The whole fucking place erupted like a frigging volcano. Mr Mafri went beserk. Mum and me could hear him throwing things around, breaking stuff. And his poor sister was howling because the family theatened to pack her back to Malta if she didn't give the guy up.'

'Did she?' I asked tentatively, aware in the corners of my mind of something being made clearer to me, something I'd rather had not been exposed.

'What would you have done, Martinesi, if your family threatened to send you packing back to a country you'd spent years trying to get away from?'

I shrugged my shoulders, knowing full well what my parents – or my father at least – would do to Rose if he ever found out about Chris the Greek. I walked on a few paces and then realised Nathan wasn't following.

'It isn't always the other guy's fault, you know,' he said.

He was right, of course. I'd always imagined the struggle being one-way, the migrants in a desperate struggle to survive amongst the natives. But there weren't any natives apart from the Aborigines, and I'd met precious few of them to draw any conclusions, and my parents and their friends would have met even fewer. The blinkers were, I suddenly realised, of our own making.

'So, you reckon he'll be back?' I asked.

For what seemed like ages Nathan didn't reply, then he caught up with me and asked, 'Do you reckon people should have to take responsibility for their own decisions, Martinesi?'

The question threw me and I shrugged my shoulders pathetically. 'I dunno,' I managed to get out finally.

'Well then, I guess you better keep praying, Martinesi, keep praying.'

12

Without really intending to, Nathan and I wound up at Fernando's.

It was much as it had been on my first visit, loud, dense with smoke, and stuffy. I thought maybe we'd meet Ralph there. We didn't, but there was someone there whose voice I recognised.

'Fuck off outta here, Welsh, you Irish prick.' It was the warehouse voice.

Nathan stopped short and I pulled up behind him. Something inside me ran to water. Around the billiard tables stood six or seven guys, all dressed in black T-shirts, black skin-tight jeans and battered black boots. Each of them had the same haircut, really short along the back and sides and nest-like on top, heavy over the forehead. With them were two girls, who were about Rose's age. They wore short black skirts over bare legs and bare feet, and, like those of the boys, their T-shirts were black, but with one striking difference: a stark silver lightning bolt was embroidered over the left breast. They had all turned to look when Ralph's brother called to us.

Nathan shifted on the balls of his feet and glanced at me quickly over his shoulder. I didn't know quite where to look so I stared directly ahead, right into the face of the taller of the two girls.

'Whatareya starin' at, Mario?' she snapped.

'He's lookin' at ya tits, Sandy,' the second girl said.

The boys around the billiard table smirked and looked at one another conspiratorially.

'Have a real good look, ya pervert,' Sandy said, and she thrust her chest out at me as I struggled to find something else to look at.

'Let's just get out,' Nathan whispered. When he made to turn on his heels, two of the group broke rank and blocked our exit.

The men at the window glanced over, chewed disinterestedly and went back to their card game.

'Where's the retard?' Ralph's brother asked. His mates laughed.

'If you mean Ralph, I dunno,' Nathan answered, not taking his eyes off the two who had moved in on either side of us. Their eyes were vacant as though they weren't in tune with the head they occupied.

'I thought you and the shithead were bum chums,' Ralph's brother went on, drawing more laughter. 'Where one cheek goes the other goes too, ain't that the way, Welsh, you Irish turd?'

Nathan shook his head, 'If you say so, Ben.'

'Yeah, I *do* say so.'

My tongue wouldn't function. I didn't want to believe Nathan's fear.

'You didn't come here to shoot pool, did ya, Welshie?' Ben asked incredulously. He looked at his mates. 'Should we let these two shitheads play?' he called.

Just then Fernando sidled over to the bar and asked if there was a problem.

'Not a one, Fred,' Ben smiled. 'Our mates here are about to shout us a drink, so line 'em up, Fred.' Then to both of the girls, 'Get us a pack o' smokes, bitch.'

Rose would've snapped right back if ever anyone dared call her 'bitch', but these girls didn't flinch. They pushed past Nathan and me, the one named Sandy blowing me a loud kiss as they went out the door.

'Why go? I got cigarettes here,' Fernando said.

'You charge too much, Freddie-boy,' Ben shot back, then returned to Nathan. 'What about if you and your wog mate there play ...' He paused a moment to glance round the billiard table, 'You twerps play me and Tag. Loser buys a hit.'

I must have said something under my breath because a moment later Ben was standing toe-to-toe with me, staring me down.

'You don't think that's fair?' he asked threateningly.

'He's clean,' Nathan interjected. 'We'll play. Loser buys a hit.'

'Sure you'll play,' Ben grinned. 'You're dumb, but not that dumb.'

Seemingly appeased, Ben called off his two dead-eyed meatheads and got them to fetch cues for Nathan and me.

'Your shout,' he told Nathan, and Nathan obliged. Fernando passed round the Cokes he'd spiked with grappa.

Back with the cigarettes, the girls took great pleasure in my anguish, and made up a new name for me, christening me Flat-arse every time I bent over to take a long shot down the table.

'But I reckon Welshie likes his arses that way,' Ben sneered at every opportunity. 'Ain't that right, Welshie?'

I looked at Nathan but he ignored me, keeping his eyes averted.

'The retard's gonna be really upset now that you got a new bum chum, Welshie,' Ralph's brother mocked. 'But then I guess the deadshit doesn't really understand what's going on, so it don't matter, eh. Maybe you three could start a club. Yeah, that's it . . . That's it. You guys could get together and call yourselves "The Deadshits".'

Ben's mates laughed, egging him on with wolf whistles and banging the top of the table.

'You'd know all about that, Ben,' Nathan said slowly and stepped just in front of me.

Ben continued laughing. 'You're lucky I'm in a good mood, Welshie, otherwise I'd rip your fucking head off and shove it up your arse.'

Nathan and I lost the game of course. Nathan played some mean shots. It was me who stuffed up the game, potting the white twice and sinking the wrong ball on a missed rebound. Nathan kept his cool.

It hurt me to see that. Despite everything, I wanted Nathan to snap, to bite back, to have a go at Ben. I wanted this even though I knew we'd probably both get our heads kicked in. But Nathan had just kept playing, once in a while suggesting a shot, but otherwise not saying anything.

We were back out in the street when Ben threatened us. 'Get this much clear, Welsh. This place is outta bounds to The Deadshit Club. I catch any of you in here again and I'm gonna forget who you are. Understand?'

Nathan didn't answer but pushed me ahead of him. In my bones I felt embarrassed for him.

'There's no way I'm going to be there tonight,' I fumed at Nathan when we'd crossed the road and were almost at the creek. 'If being in Fernando's doesn't get me killed by my parents, getting involved in a dope drop will.'

'Listen, Martinesi,' Nathan seethed, his anger and humiliation now rising to the surface. 'I know Ben enough to know this much. We *both* took on the bet and we *both* lost. Now he expects *both* of us to front up. For your own sake, Martinesi, play it safe and meet me outside Mafris' just before eleven. I know where we can score some dope cheap. It isn't great stuff, but by the time Ben and his mates get it they'll be so pissed they'll think it's gold . . .

'Look,' he continued without looking at me. 'Ben's really screwed up. He doesn't think the way me and you do. You fuck with him and he comes back at you with a hundred times as much. All that crap about 'The Deadshit Club', it was just his way of getting me – or you – to push the right button so he'd have a reason to go ballistic in there. You with me?'

'Yeah, I'm with you,' I grunted, unconvinced. This wasn't what I'd expected of Nathan Welsh.

Nathan was still behind me as we came up out of the creek bank and within sight of the silos. 'You think I chickened out back there, don't you, Martinesi?' he called at my back. 'You reckon I should have told Ben and his deadheads to stick it.'

I turned and shrugged my shoulders. 'I don't know what you should have done.'

'Yeah right, Martinesi, You never know bloody anything.' Nathan smirked. He had stopped and was standing with his arms folded. 'You don't know a thing about me or Ralph or Ben, Martinesi. You think you do, but you know jackshit about us. And that's a fact.'

'So tell me more then,' I demanded

Nathan dropped his arms and faced me. 'You got anything you'd like to get off your chest, Martinesi?' he asked so slowly his words hung in the air between us. 'You don't have to come tonight, Martinesi,' he continued before I could respond. 'I'll go for us. You get some sleep.'

Nathan walked on ahead.

I don't know how long I stood there watching his back as he walked on, but I slowly realised that I had to go with him that night. I had no choice. Nathan had committed us both.

I'd never had to make a decision like that before. Commitments, consequences; they belonged to other people, people like Nathan Welsh who imposed their own rules on things. Or at least acknowledged their responsibilities. It suddenly dawned on me that this was how Nathan survived at St Joe's. He was committed to being there. He took full responsibility for his presence at the old blue pile, and if he wasn't able to do it academically, he did it through his sporting achievements, his tenacity, his determination to be noticed.

I wanted to tell Nathan as much but instead when I caught up with him I told him what I'd overheard and seen at the warehouse. Nathan listened without interrupting me or asking a single question. When I got to the part about Ralph running off in tears I saw Nathan flinch and I almost wished I'd said nothing at all.

'It wouldn't be the first time,' Nathan informed me. 'Ben's always into Ralph for one thing or another. Worse since their mum died about a year back. She was a pretty decent lady too, Ralph's mum. My old lady and her used to go to school together. She and Mum and Ralph and me would sometimes do things together. The odd trip into town to catch a movie, maybe a pizza now and then. She – Ralph's mum – used to take real special care of Ralph, never let him out of her sight, always watching over him. It's a fact, Ralph's always been kind of slow on the uptake you know. Everything takes a little longer with Ralph.

'But he's bloody good with his hands, Ralph. He can draw and carve and do all sorts of arty shit Ben and me are useless at. But the old man was – is – a real bastard. He drinks like a fish and does nothing much besides. He never let Ralph help out around the house, never let him help with the car or anything. Not like Ben. Ben got to bang nails, paint the fence, saw wood, the works.

'Ralph has never got anything off his old man, nothing. Not like Ben. The old man and Ben were real mates for a time. I guess that's why me and Ralph got to spend so much time together. I didn't have an old man by then and Ralph as good as didn't. And then his old lady develops some tumour on the brain and just stops living . . . just sorta goes into a coma and dies . . .'

Nathan led the way over some vacant land.

'What would you have done in my place? About Ralph and Ben I mean, there at the warehouse?' I asked quickly, afraid that if I hesitated the question would evaporate off my tongue.

'If you mean, would I have gone up against Ben, no, I wouldn't have,' Nathan answered, lighting a cigar. 'No point in that. Ben doesn't fight fair. Before I'd have got a punch in, his deadheads would have mashed my face to a pulp. If you mean after Ralph had been tossed out, I probably would have hung my head in shame. You see, Martinesi, my job is to stop Ralph getting into trouble *before* it happens.' He dropped his voice. 'That's what I promised his mum. And most times I can because I kind of know Ralph's ways now . . .'

I was puzzled and said so. 'But you're not always around.'

'True,' Nathan nodded, 'but while he's with Mr Gaglieri

he's cool. Mr Gaglieri knew his mum and he knows how to handle Ralph. As for when I'm away, like the last few weeks – ' Nathan screwed up his face as though in pain. 'I'm no miracle worker, Martinesi. And anyway, he usually goes off on camp every year. His mum arranged it years ago through Father D'Ambriosa and some welfare group. They usually pick Ralph up just after Christmas Day and have him home just on the New Year. This year the camp was suddenly cancelled, just before school finished.'

My ears pricked up. I stopped walking. Nathan kept talking, his face turned away from me.

'Sometimes even the best laid plans screw up,' he continued. 'I never figured you'd go off on a holiday, Martinesi. Never in a million years. But what could I do, you're the only one I reckon I'd trust Ralph to . . .'

I found my voice, 'You mean you set me up? You planned for me and Ralph to meet so that I could . . . I could babysit him while you went off on your holiday?'

'Relax, Martinesi,' Nathan said. 'It's Ralph we're talking about here. When I heard the camp wasn't on I needed to find someone I could rely on, someone with some commonsense, with . . . with a bit of heart, who might just keep an eye open for Ralph – '

'CRAP!' I yelled and felt my eyes almost pop with the effort. 'You just wanted a babysitter for some stupid bastard retard who – '

Nathan punched me so hard on the mouth I left the ground, and landed with a thud, my back just short of the water.

'Ralph isn't a bastard, Martinesi,' Nathan yelled as he stood over me. 'And he's not a retard. You got that, Martinesi?'

I swallowed, blood tickling my throat.

Nothing stirred.

'Get up, Martinesi,' Nathan ordered quietly, reaching towards me. I took his hand and stumbled groggily to my feet. My jaw and neck rang with pain.

'I . . . I'm sorry,' I slurred.

'Nah, it's me who's sorry,' Nathan replied. 'I'm sorry about getting you involved with Ralph and Ben and the drug shit. Don't worry about tonight, I'll handle it.'

He turned to go, but a moment later, his hand outstretched, said, 'You wanna give me back that key.'

I touched my lip. It stung and was still bleeding. I suddenly remembered how I'd felt that first time on the silos. I remembered Zio Paul and the crap he'd put up with.

'Can we meet somewhere other than the Mafris'?' I asked through a mouthful of spit.

Nathan grinned, shook his head, 'Don't go trying to be a hero, Martinesi.'

'What about Ralph? Where d'you reckon he's got to?'

'How'll you explain your fat lip?' Nathan asked, changing the subject.

I shrugged. 'I fell out of a tree.'

We both laughed.

'Shit that hurts,' I moaned. 'You reckon Ralph's okay?' I asked after a moment.

'Yeah, Ralph's fine. He was waiting for me the minute I got home. He's like a loyal pup that guy.' When I didn't laugh Nathan slung an arm around my shoulders and gave me a jab on the side of the face. 'You know, Ralph told me all about his run-in with Ben, about how he'd backed out of their plan to clean Gaglieri out. And you were right, Martinesi, they did slap him about.' Nathan paused and looked at me, not hard, but closely. 'He saw you, you know,' he told me softly.

I pulled away. Nathan let me go.

'He saw you at the window,' he went on. 'Don't worry, no one else did. And Ralph ain't the type to tell on a mate, either. Ralph told me basically what you did, except that he gave me more of the details about Ben and Tag's plan to ransack the workshop, take what they could unload easily at second-hand shops, the markets, whatever, and put Gaglieri on notice about rethinking Ben's proposal to have half of Ralph's pay paid directly to him "for the sake of me brother's future". Can you believe that crap?

'I'm proud of you, Martinesi, for telling me about that shit-kicker Ben and what you'd overheard. I wondered whether you would, you know, given as how you didn't go after Ralph or anything.'

'So where is he now?' I asked, angry that Nathan hadn't told me earlier. It wasn't a betrayal exactly but it hurt to have been tested.

'Ralph? He's at work of course. Where else did you expect him to be, Martinesi?'

You had to laugh, I told myself, otherwise everything was just too serious, too nerve-shattering. So I did. I laughed loudly, recklessly, my head thrown up at the sky, eyes closed. My laughter carried like thunder up towards the tops of the silos.

'You okay, Martinesi?'

'All I ever wanted was to go on a *real* holiday,' I spluttered, 'just *one* holiday like a normal kid, rather than the same tired wasted weeks of watching TV, painting the spouting, driving out to St Kilda beach in the back seat of the wog-wagon. Endless, boring bloody days.

'And what do I get? I get a commissioned friendship with a guy who pops up in my back yard asking for a snag, a perve at a naked woman whose skin looks like dry parchment, and a fat lip from the kid who's spent most of the past two years on my back because I was a daggy wog stay-at-home. You gotta admit, Nathan, life's pretty fucked . . .'

'Yeah,' Nathan snorted. 'Life's pretty fucked all right, but at least we're not Ben . . .'

13

On Nathan's insistence we were waiting for Ralph when he got off work. Ralph seemed happy to see me and gave me the thumbs up.

'You're back, Dave,' he said cheerfully.

'Guess so.'

Ralph put an arm around me and slapped me playfully on the back of the head. 'He's got a great bike,' he told Nathan. 'One day I'm gonna buy me a bike like that too. Then me and Dave'll go ride together. We'll be mates, the two of us – like me and Nathan. Buddies.'

'Yeah, well, for now you just try thinking about saving your dough and keeping out of trouble,' Nathan said, grinning.

Ralph nodded – too readily, I thought – then pulled a packet of chips from the pocket of his overalls and plunged right into them.

'You might just like to chew one or two of those, Ralph,' Nathan laughed, winking at me. 'If he ever offers you a chip, don't get your hand in the way or he's likely to bite the bloody thing off. Just loves chips, he does. Chips and sausages. Don't you, Ralph?'

Ralph paused, his hand poised halfway between his mouth and the chip packet. 'I never got to finish lunch. We was busy,' he said by way of explanation, then went back to shovelling the chips into his mouth.

Nathan rolled his eyes and I laughed into my hand.

How odd, I thought, that Nathan should take so much interest in this lanky kid who seemed not altogether there. They were a strange duo. But we were an even stranger trio, so what did it matter? Maybe Zio Paul had been right after all.

'Martinesi reckons he got to perve on a couple screwing while he was on holidays,' Nathan said, taking Ralph's work bag from him and looking inside. 'Didn't you, Martinesi. And the bird had great big tits and an even bigger arse,' Nathan laughed. 'Tell him, Martinesi. Tell him about how your dick grew so long you had to tie it in a knot to get it back into your jocks.'

I ignored Nathan's jibes, curious why he seemed to be checking Ralph's bag for something. 'What are you looking for?' I asked.

Nathan hesitated for a moment. 'What's today, Ralph?' he asked.

'Pay day,' Ralph replied.

'And what do we have to do on pay day, Ralph?'

Ralph licked his fingers and looked first at me and then at Nathan as though unsure what to say.

'Ralph?' Nathan pressed, 'what do we do on pay day?' He was talking to Ralph, but I sensed that Nathan was, in fact, addressing me.

Ralph stiffened a little. 'Me and you make sure my money's all put away right,' he said. 'Gotta check that all the money's in the book.'

Nathan smiled. 'Yep. We have to check that Ben hasn't

put the hard word on Mr Gaglieri about him banking your money for you.' Nathan held up a pay slip and waved it in my direction. 'We have to keep making sure the money goes straight into the bank where Ben can't get his hands on it, don't we Ralph?'

Ralph beamed, obviously satisfied that he'd got the answer right, and Nathan smiled warmly.

'Got to look out for each other,' Ralph said sing-song fashion. 'Got to keep your head up and your eyes open. Got to listen with two ears. Got to – '

'Right, thanks Ralph,' Nathan said, cutting him off. 'We've got the general idea.' Then to me, 'He's an easy target, you know.' And with that Nathan handed Ralph back his work bag and we walked on.

That's when I decided it was probably time to apologise to Ralph about what had happened at the warehouse. 'Ralph, about your brother roughing you up – '

'Shut up about that,' Nathan growled. 'It's over with, okay, Martinesi? It's done. So just shut up about it.' Then to Ralph, who had edged away, 'It's all right, mate. He won't tell anyone.'

We stood in silence then, with me looking from Nathan to Ralph and back again, too afraid to utter another word for fear of saying something else out of place. Ralph blinked blankly and grimaced.

Nathan poked him in the ribs. 'Guess what me and Martinesi did this afternoon?' he asked. 'We shot pool with Ben and Tag . . . and lost.' Nathan was laughing thinly. 'The two of us, we've got to settle a little debt with them later tonight.'

Ralph shifted his weight from foot to foot.

'The usual shit, Ralph,' Nathan added, a touch of uncertainty in his voice. 'You know what it's like. Ben's so irresistible you can't help playing pool with him when he invites you to.'

Ralph's face seemed to have collapsed and he stared at me.

'It's all right, Ralph,' Nathan whispered, 'Martinesi won't say anything about what happened at the warehouse. I promise. Isn't that right, Martinesi?'

There was something hard and cold in my belly again. 'Yeah, I ... I guess so ... I never – '

Nathan put a hand up to stop me. 'And anyway,' he said stiffly, 'If Ben ever heard a whisper he'd use Martinesi's balls for shooting pool.'

Ralph looked at me and seemed to close in on himself even more. 'Dad's home,' he said so softly I could barely hear him. 'I ... I gotta get home, Nathan. Dad's at home, and he's waiting for me so ...'

'Ralph!' Nathan called when Ralph turned to go. 'Ralph?'

But Ralph ran off with a quick wave.

'You're not going after him?' I asked Nathan.

'Nah,' he said flatly. 'He probably just had another fight with his old man last night and has to get in early tonight.'

I looked hard at Nathan but his face betrayed nothing.

Nathan was alone when we met up outside the Mafris' milk bar much later that night.

'Ralph not coming with us?' I asked, thinking it unusual that Nathan would not include him.

'This hasn't got anything to do with Ralph,' Nathan snapped.

I had just climbed out of my bedroom window, crept out along the side of the house and past the silos in the middle of the night, and I wasn't about to be snapped at for no good reason. 'Look Nathan, if you're blaming me for upsetting

Ralph by mentioning what happened at the warehouse I reckon you're nuts. You said yourself he'd seen me so what difference did it make if I mentioned it?'

But Nathan was in no mood to answer and he set off down the street.

'I'm not real sure I know what's up with you and Ralph,' I said as we walked, hugging the walls where the shadows were deepest. 'I don't even know for sure what I'm doing out here in the middle of the night, scared shitless that one of my folks will go in to check up on me and find the bed empty, following some guy who took a great deal of pleasure in tormenting me not that long ago.

'You have to say the whole thing is pretty bizarre,' I continued. 'What reason have I got to go putting my neck on the line by coming out on a dope drop to a couple of space cadets, one of whom has a brother I'm not all that convinced understands exactly what the hell is going on around him ...'

Nathan stopped suddenly and turned, his eyes narrow and dark. 'Martinesi, you talk a lot but you don't really say all that much,' he said. 'At least with Ralph what little he does say actually means something. And I'll tell you this much, Martinesi. You don't know shit about humiliation or being tormented, or even what it might be like to be a real outsider. Keep your mouth shut, eyes open, ears tuned and you might just learn something ...

'Whatever was on Ralph's mind this afternoon had nothing to do with you, Martinesi. Whatever he was thinking about after you mentioned the warehouse had nothing to do with your attempted apology ...' Nathan lowered his voice. 'I went by Ralph's before meeting you, and he wasn't home. His old man was too pissed to notice and so I don't know where he is right now.' There was concern in Nathan's voice, like that day at the silos when Ralph had walked out to retrieve Nathan's gear.

. I felt ashamed all of a sudden. 'You reckon he's okay?' I asked, chastened.

Nathan shrugged, 'Hope so. I wish I knew what was bugging him, though.'

Nathan and I had just decided not to wait any longer for Ben and his mates to show when a wail of sirens drew us away from the warehouse. There was a glow we hadn't noticed, because we were too intent on looking out for Ralph's brother and his gang. We moved towards it, trailing the sirens.

It was Nathan who identified the source of the glow. He looked at me, his eyes suddenly piercing. Around us the sirens wailed and shrieked, and the street seemed to swell with their sounds. The glow settled on the sky just behind where the silos rose dark and imposing.

'Shit,' I said, taking in the eerie light show. 'Must be a massive fire.'

Nathan didn't seem to hear me. He cocked his head and squinted at the smoke that was wafting overhead.

'No!'

I heard his whisper a fraction of a second before he started sprinting down the middle of the street, arms tearing at his sides.

By the time I caught up to Nathan we had run the few short blocks to Ralph's workplace. Flames roared out from every shattered window and doorway. Black smoke billowed in dense plumes that hid the moon overhead and drifted across the street to where Nathan and I hung on the edge of disbelief.

We knew.

We knew like we knew that come dawn the night would evaporate away. Nathan and I knew the where, the how and the why of the fire. But we didn't know where Ralph was.

'Nathan?' I called, as though he might put some meaning into what was going on.

'They've torched it! They fucking torched it,' was all I heard him say over and over as the two of us stood paralysed amongst the gawkers and sightseers.

The roof suddenly caved in, and an explosion of wind, fire and crumbling masonry sent me sprawling backwards.

And only then did I see the still smoking bundles of charred remains on the road, remains that someone at that very moment was covering with sheets and blankets.

'Nathan,' I heard myself saying from somewhere deep inside where I lay apart from what I was seeing. 'Nathan.' But I couldn't say anything other than his name.

It was as if Nathan no longer existed.

I knew then. I knew without having to run up and peer into the blackened mass.

I knew it as a pinpoint of pain in the very centre of my chest, a pinpoint of pain that made my hair stand on end.

This was the beginning of the nightmare images of faceless forms running in blind panic from barred window to barred window in a futile attempt to escape the blaze they had set off to cover their crime.

In those tortuous hours we stood numb with hopelessness, looking on as the flames were extinguished and the place was cordoned off, Nathan and I were as ghosts to one another. We didn't say a word, speech stolen from us by disbelief.

And there were no words as we ran from that place, no

words that might have reached across the enormous gulf that had become the space between where Nathan and I had stood.

I ran at Nathan's side, mouth open to catch every possible whisper of air that might wash the taste of acrid smoke and ash out of my mouth, flush it from my nostrils.

The sky above us bled for Ralph, the sulphur moon at our backs peeping out from behind the last flutes of smoke as Nathan and I ran and ran and ran.

It's easy to run a marathon and not experience pain when the devil chases you. I'd heard that from my Nonna many times. You just keep running beyond yourself, forcing yourself out of your skin so that flesh and bones might be chasing each other in turn.

That's how it was for me and Nathan. We ran with a shadow hovering at our backs through deserted streets that led everywhere and nowhere, down back lanes where dogs and cats scattered before us or huddled tense and frightened in our wake. Past the warehouse where nothing much stirred but the restless junkies too out of it to notice us. And on past the silos, their steel lids iridescent above us, seeming to loom closer to earth than to heaven.

My thoughts were of nothing specific; that's all I can say with any clarity. My mind was a confusion of a thousand different thoughts, none of them sharp enough to stay with me longer than an instant. None, that is, except the too vivid realisation that nothing could ever again be how it had been; not before the fire, not before the holiday . . . not before meeting Ralph.

As we ran past the back fence of my house it was all too obvious that its walls weren't the only barrier between the rest of my family and me any more.

Nathan and I kept running until finally we collapsed in

shaking heaps under a canopy of willows that cocooned us in its light and shade, real and unreal.

I've often thought about it since that night, that last time Nathan and I saw Ralph. A million times I've blamed Nathan and myself for not insisting Ralph tell us what was bothering him, for not following him all the way home, for not pressing him as to why he had to get home when, on any other day, Ralph would have been more than glad to hang out away from there for as long as possible.

In the long days and nights that followed the identification of Ralph's charred body in the ruins of Gaglieri's French Polish and Cabinet-making Services, all sense of right and wrong, up and down, past and present became lost behind an overwhelming sense of futility and pain. A pain that made my bones ache.

14

Ralph is dead. Ralph is dead.

Ralph is dead, I told myself over and over and over again.

I woke up and shouted into the twisted canopy overhead. 'RALPH IS DEAD!'

When I stared about me I saw that Nathan was asleep beside me, his face ravaged with pain.

For an instant I wanted to believe in my dream as just that, a dream – cruel and savage and terrifying but ultimately benign.

'Can you believe this shit,' I said out loud, waking Nathan. I told him my nightmare, words tumbling ahead of thoughts. 'I actually dreamt about Ralph. Do you believe how off my face I must have been to dream up that stuff ...' I laughed for my own sake, my eyes floating, drifting from one empty beer stubbie to another where they lay at our feet. I couldn't remember where they'd come from, though I did vaguely recall Nathan going off for them at some stage (before or after we'd smoked the dope?), returning with so much grog that he walked hunched over. I didn't even bother asking him where he'd got it all. He was Nathan Welsh after all, procurer of marijuana and all things needed or desired.

'What're we going to do?' I whispered pathetically.

Nathan didn't answer. He just sat there next to me, head between his knees, gently rocking back and forth.

'We let him down,' Nathan said finally. 'He relied on us to be his mates and we let him down.'

I kicked at an empty beer bottle lying at my feet. It spun and rolled into the creek. I was fully awake now. My head whirled, and my eyes darted in and out of their sockets. I closed them and lay down, arms flung across my face. Nathan sobbed breathlessly. 'Did you see . . . ? Did you see what was left?' he stammered. 'Nothing . . . Nothing but bones and . . .'

The rawness in my throat made swallowing painful, like gulping shredded glass.

'What're we gonna do?' I asked again as I tried to get to my feet. I folded over onto my side, weak and nauseated. I burped and burped into the cool onion weed, my face running with saliva, beer and God-only-knew-what.

'He was my best mate, my best friend,' Nathan said to someone other than me. When I looked up of course no one else was there. I let him go on.

'I should've realised something was wrong. I should've seen it in his face. He was scared, shit scared of something, or someone. Ben most probably. And I didn't see it . . . I mean I did, I did see it, but I didn't do anything about it.'

Nathan pushed himself down to the creek and splashed water over his face, keeping his back to me. 'Ralph idolised Ben, but he was shit scared of him . . . Scared to death of his brother. Ben was always looking for ways to humiliate Ralph, to tease him, get him to do really stupid or sick things . . .'

Like on the silos that first day, I thought suddenly, aware of the chill in Nathan's tone. Surely he wasn't implying that he still held me responsible for Ralph's stunt on the silos that day when he'd gone after Nathan's things?

'Maybe . . . Maybe it wasn't Ralph back there,' I said. But of course it *was* Ralph on the road there outside the burning ruins of the workshop. That *was* Ralph's corpse on the road and we both knew it.

'YES, IT'S RALPH,' Nathan screamed, turning to face me, the muscles in his neck bulging. 'IT'S RALPH AND HE'S DEAD, AND WE LET IT HAPPEN . . . ME AND YOU AND THE OLD MAN. YOU HEAR ME, MARTINESI, YOU STUPID WOG? RALPH'S DEAD. WELCOME TO THE OTHER SIDE.'

Nathan strode past me and I watched as he climbed the bank at my back.

'Nathan.' I cried at his back, 'Nathan, where're you going? . . . NATHAN! . . . WELSH! . . . NATHAN! . . . WHERE'RE YOU GOING, FUCK YOU?'

But Nathan didn't reply. I started cursing him, lapsing from English to Italian and back again.

'THIS ISN'T HOW IT'S SUPPOSED TO BE, WELSH!' I yelled until my lungs hurt. 'THIS IS JUST A BAD JOKE . . . A BAD JOKE, YOU HEAR ME WELSH? YOU HEAR ME? THERE IS NO OTHER SIDE NATHAN WELSH, YOU IRISH TURD!' I yelled into the water, and into the bank opposite. 'There is no other side. There's no other side and you're a fake, Nathan Welsh. You're a phoney and a fake and a fraud.'

I fell back onto the grass, exhausted. I don't know how long I lay there after Nathan had gone. It might have been a few minutes or a few hours. Nothing made any sense. I know I wanted to get up. Yet every time I made a move to sit up my head took flight and the world rose and fell around me. I fell into a fitful sleep and woke with a start. I sat up too quickly, throwing up all over myself.

I had to get home. Mum and Dad would know what to do. That's where I ought to have gone in the first place. Home. Mum and Dad would have known what to do, what to say, where to go.

I had to get home.

Who did I think I was?

I had to tell Mum and Dad what I'd seen. And not just about the fire, but Ralph's humiliation at the warehouse, what I'd heard. They had to know. Had to know so they could tell me what to do, what to say –

A noise at my back made me look round guiltily. Who had I expected to see – Ralph?

It was Nathan. His face was ashen, his eyes hollow.

'They've taken him away,' he announced flatly. 'Ben and Tag as well.'

I faced the water and tried not to look at Nathan.

'I wanted to convince myself it wasn't him,' Nathan went on behind me. 'I went to his place but the cops were already there. Seems the rest of Ben's gang were the ones who called for help when the fire broke out. The cops knew who to break the news to because Sandy went screaming to them at the scene that her boyfriend Tag was in the building. From that the cops found out about Ben and – and Ralph.

'The old man's pissed. When I got to the house two cops were helping him out of bed. I don't even reckon he heard a word they told him, not about Ralph, or Ben, or the fire.' Anger crept into Nathan's voice, 'The old bastard's so drunk he probably doesn't even know his boys are missing. Not that that's anything new. The old man never gave a shit about them anyhow. Not about Ralph. Not about Ben. Not about anyone but himself.'

'A bit like you I guess, hey,' I blurted out and immediately wished I hadn't. I knew how unfair those words were. I wanted to look at Nathan but I didn't have the guts. Instead I stepped heavily into the shallows of the creek and splashed water onto my jeans to rinse off the vomit.

I waited for Nathan to speak, half expecting him to push me over into the oil-smeared water.

'You're one to talk, Martinesi, with your cosy cocoon family wrapping you in so much loving cottonwool you don't even see that people like Ralph exist,' he said after a while. 'What gives you the right to feel sorry for Ralph, eh? You don't know shit about Ralph or why he was in that fire last night.'

He was standing to my left now, staring at me, his body tense and rigid.

'Yeah that's right, Martinesi, Ben was Ralph's *half*-brother. Same piss-pot old man, different mum. You starting to get the picture, Martinesi? You starting to see the light? Why d'you reckon Ralph's mum was so keen for me to look out for him? Don't you reckon she should've asked his own brother to look out for Ralph? You'd think so wouldn't you? But you see, Martinesi, there was no way she could ask Ben to keep an eye on Ralph. And you know what, Martinesi, even though Ralph's dead I'm still glad his mum didn't arrange to have him put away in a home. You never know, he might have turned out like you, Martinesi – scared of the fucking shadows.'

I pounced on Nathan with all the strength I could muster and knocked him to the ground. We rolled and tumbled, limbs entwined, gasping for air as we slid into the creek, splashing about as we tried to cough out the foul water.

When it was over we sat there in the gently lapping water and heaved with sadness.

'He's dead, Martinesi, Ralph's dead.' There was real sorrow in Nathan's voice, sorrow I couldn't remember even at the most sombre Italian funerals, where the family wailed and howled and then attempted to throw themselves into the grave along with the coffin. There was no one but me to witness Nathan's sorrow.

I didn't think I could bear it.

The creek bank whispered a million shared thoughts as Nathan and I helped each other to our feet and waded clumsily out of the water.

'I really should get you home, Martinesi,' Nathan said mock seriously after we had systematically smashed every empty beer bottle we could find.

'You mean, I'd better get you home, Welsh,' I countered. 'Your mum might be frantic with worry over you, and we can't have that, hey.'

When I got home the house was exploding with hysteria and panic. There was so much distress and anger and fear in the air that the moment I climbed over the back fence I wished some of it might have been showered on Ralph.

'Stay out of Dad's way,' Rose warned me, stopping me before I'd even reached the back door. 'He's not really thinking straight right now.'

I nodded and let Rose lead the way into the kitchen. 'Don't admit to anything. Don't tell them anything, okay. Please, for both our sakes,' she said. Then she turned and wiped something from my face, adding, 'I always thought you and Zio Paul had something in common. Now I think I know what.'

Just then I saw our mother. She was sitting at the table and her eyes had that same look of resignation I'd seen as we'd walked away from Zio Paul's bungalow.

Dad was right behind her. I could see the veins at his temples throbbing, his eyes white with rage.

I walked in and all sound, all movement was swallowed up in my wake. It was as though no one could quite believe I was there. Except Mum. Mum blinked hard at me and then pulled me to her without a word. It was she who stayed my father's blows.

'It's like Paolo all over again,' I heard my Nonna say from somewhere behind Mum, somewhere behind the cloud of confusion that swelled in my brain. But my mum's response was as clear as if I'd uttered the words myself.

'No, it's not like that at all,' she said firmly. 'This is my son, not yours.'

'You know,' Rose told me afterwards, when our father had gone for a walk to clear his head, 'Dad really began to lose it when we got news about the fire at Gaglieri's from Zio Sandro. When Dad heard that bodies had been pulled out from the blaze and that the remains were unrecognisable . . .'

Rose blinked down at the floor before adding, 'Mum didn't want to believe it might be you in that fire. She just kept saying that wherever you were, you weren't in that fire . . .'

'What about you, Rose, what did you think?' I asked.

'I had a feeling you'd be with Nathan Welsh,' she replied. 'You two and . . . and Ralph, just seemed to suddenly have this thing about hanging out together. I kinda wondered at the coincidence of you making friends with Welsh and you going missing without a word – '

'What did you tell Mum and Dad?'

Rose blinked softly, the way Nonna did when she felt you should let something alone, then said, 'I told Mum you'd told me that Zio Paul's leaving had really upset you, and that you just needed some time to yourself to sort it all out. I told her I knew where you were, that you were all right and that you'd be home soon. I also told her not to tell Dad that story because he'd go nuts at Zio Paul – '

'So she told Dad she didn't know where I was?' I cut in, surprised but not startled at having Rose as an ally.

Rose shook her head, 'No, Mum told Dad that you and her had argued and that you'd threatened to storm off, but that she was sure you'd be back – and soon – '

'And he bought that?' I asked incredulously.

'Not at first, but eventually I guess. Although he preferred to believe you'd got yourself involved with a slut or something.'

'Do you reckon Mum believed you, Rose?' I asked, even though the answer was written all over her face.

'About Zio Paul? No,' she replied with a shrug. 'She knew I was covering for you. Not that she said as much, but – '

'Her look, right.'

'Yeah, her look,' Rose affirmed. 'She just kind of looked through me. It was pretty scary.'

'And you knew that she knew more than you'd said.'

Rose nodded. 'Other than the fire, she was just too cool, too controlled. I couldn't believe it.'

I could, because of that visit to Zio Paul with Mum. And I knew now why she'd taken me along, and why she'd told me what she had about her younger brother. She was not about to repeat the sins of her own mother.

Nathan and his mum went to Ralph's funeral. He told me that the two of them sat up front where family should have been but weren't.

I would like to have gone to the funeral, but I couldn't bring myself to go. There was a hard core of pain inside me that didn't want to have to face up to the thought of whatever remained of Ralph lying there inside the coffin.

'You should come you know, Martinesi,' Nathan had told me. 'For Ralph's sake, you should be there.'

But I wasn't. And all the while I knew the service was on I sat in my room, wishing I could shut out the world.

Rose came in and sat with me, not saying anything, just sitting at the end of my bed, her head bowed, breathing quietly and slowly.

'He was a pretty good kid,' I said finally, unable to sit there in silence any longer. 'He didn't deserve to die the way he did.'

And that was it. There was nothing else I could say. Ralph was dead. I was alive, but no longer living in a sheltered world where everyone I knew at least had someone who really cared about them.

At that moment I would have given almost anything to have been able to talk to my Zio Paul. Of everyone apart from Nathan, he would have understood Ralph and why Ralph and Nathan had become so much a part of my life. And maybe he might have been able to explain it to me.

15

'Did you know Nonna refuses to sleep with her back to the door?' Rose asked me as we took turns ladling the freshly squeezed tomato sauce into the sterilised beer bottles Dad had collected since our last sauce-making day. 'She reckons if death's going to come at night she wants to look him right in the eye.'

'How does she know death is a male?' I asked.

'The same way some man decided God was a male,' Rose said. 'But anyway, she spends a good half-hour brushing her hair before she goes to bed. It's like, one hair at a time please. Got to look good for death.'

Nonna, who was hacking the tomatoes in half, made one of her farting sounds and leaned an elbow on one knee. 'If I die Rosa, I don't want to go to my grave looking like death warmed up.'

Rose and I stared at each other. You just didn't know how much English Nonna could understand, even if she always replied in Italian.

'You'll live for a hundred years,' Mum said from where she was hunched over the grinder.

'If my children continue to give me heartaches I won't live to see tomorrow,' Nonna complained. Mum replied with a slow shake of her head and a reminder that Nonna was welcome to stay with us until she felt more comfortable about returning to her own home.

'My home is in Italy,' Nonna said, pointing a bony finger in the general direction she must have thought Italy lay. 'Not even as a corpse will I ever go back. I came here to live, and here I'll die and rot away.' She made her farting noise again, only this time a line of spittle ran down the corner of her mouth. 'See,' she said, wiping it away. 'You leave your land behind and before you know it you turn into a useless bag of bones ...'

Rose rolled her eyes.

'Rosa!' Dad shouted and Rose huffed and returned to the tomatoes, muttering, 'You'd think the Australian government forced her to come out here.' Luckily for Rose no one seemed to have heard.

I decided I had nothing to lose. 'What was Zio Paolo like at my age?' I asked Nonna.

I saw Nonna shift uncomfortably on her stool. She continued hacking at the tomato in her hand, then a second, and a third.

'He was a boy,' she answered at her leisure, her voice steady. 'He went to school and did enough to pass one year to the next. He wasn't so clever like you, Davide, but he was clever enough for a boy who had to learn a strange new language that he could not use at home with his mama.

'Paolo had to grow up the baby of the family. He had a sister he hadn't seen for a few years, and an older brother who had too much responsibility put on his shoulders when he was much too young for it. He was not the breadwinner, and he was not the one I had time to dote on because after your grandfather died I had to do what I could to make us survive. I couldn't just let poor Sandro carry all the burden, not after Teresa came out here.'

Nonna stopped hacking at the tomatoes and crossed herself. 'Your Nonno would have been very proud of his children.'

'Even of Zio Paolo?'

'Even of my Paolo,' she replied flatly.

'Bet you're glad Zio Paolo's not a kid now, hey. There's so much stuff around now for kids to get into trouble with.' I tried to sound as casual as possible. I watched Nonna's face as we spoke. Her eyes never faltered. Even as she lied they did not betray her.

She looked past me to where Mum was looking on, her face smeared with tomato skins. 'No, he was never any trouble,' Nonna said firmly.

'Except now,' I said. I could feel Dad lurking threateningly in the shadows at my back. But I didn't care. I knew the truth. I knew it. I just wanted Nonna to tell it openly.

'He is a man now,' my Nonna replied, and set to work again. 'Men do what they believe they have to do.'

'Did you ever wish he'd settled down with a nice *paesana* girl?' I pressed.

Nonna grinned and I saw the mole on her neck jump, the loose skin flat under her stubbled chin.

'Davide,' she said softly, 'some worlds will never meet, no matter how often or how hard you may try to bring them together. Your Zio Paolo has chosen a foreign world and to that I cannot answer. Maybe one day you can ask him why a man chooses to abandon reason in favour of whim ...'

I couldn't tell her that I didn't have to ask Zio Paul, that the answer was all too obvious if she cared to look closely enough.

Later that same afternoon, while the bottles of tomato sauce slowly rattled in boiling water in the forty gallon drum, Nathan and I went to see the school principal about our idea for a Year 10 social. Naturally it was Nathan who took the idea to Brother Ignatius.

'How'd it go?' I called as Nathan ran past me after being with Brother Ig for almost half an hour.

Nathan spun round on his heels. 'Where you been?' he asked.

'In confession with The Dome,' I grinned. 'And boy, are you ever the black mark on the list.' In truth I'd only exchanged a few words with Brother Richard, who had been on his way out as I waited for Nathan in the sprawling gardens. It was true that I had mentioned that I was there with Nathan Welsh and that The Dome had been less than impressed. As The Dome put it, he was rather surprised that a boy of my good character should be spending time with the likes of a Nathan Welsh. I told Nathan as much.

'He hates me? ... Me? ... N-o-o!' Nathan said with exaggerated horror. 'And you know, I try and I try to model myself on his pious example, but you see, Martinesi – I could never bring myself to be that big a dickhead.'

'When I told him you'd come to see Brother Ig, The Dome implied you've probably got too much influence over the way things are done at St Joe's,' I added cautiously, aware that Nathan's reputation extended to whispered accounts of how Brother Ig relied on him for information about what was going on around the place.

Nathan paused in his stride and waited until I'd caught up. 'Martinesi,' he said slowly, as though measuring his words. 'Martinesi, without my footy and cricket and swimming and so on, I'd have sweet FA to show for my time at St Joe's. And Brother Ig knows that. Not just about me either. But about La Rocca, Anderson – most of the big-time heroes ... Guys like you, Martinesi, have got it all over us in the brains department ... We can't compete with you bookworms – sorry – you brainy types ... So Brother Ig does his best to let us poor dopey bastards achieve some success on the sports field, in the pool, on the track. You follow? It's a bloody con to keep guys like us at St Joe's, where guys like Brother Ig can try and weave their magic as far as God and religion are concerned. In a word, it's all bullshit, Martinesi. Bullshit.'

I walked alongside Nathan in silence, trying to make sense of what he'd said.

Nathan must have sensed my unease for he punched my arm playfully and said curtly, 'It's all a game, Martinesi. Nothing to stress out over.'

But I wasn't convinced, and I guessed that Nathan wasn't either.

It started to rain when we were in sight of the warehouse. The sky rolled over into a murky yellow–orange, clouds low and black, the sun a haze visible only now and then in the rapidly changing light that masked everything in a soft shadow.

We were closer to Nathan's place than we were to the warehouse so I stuck my neck out and suggested we take shelter at his place. After all, I told Nathan, his mum knew about me so there shouldn't be a problem.

'Except one,' Nathan countered.

'And that is?'

'Tim.' Nathan said the name in the same sharp way he uttered a curse.

'What's the problem? Doesn't he like wogs or something?'
I laughed.

Nathan walked ahead of me, leaning into the rain. 'Tim
doesn't like wogs, dogs, kids – and people in general,' he
snorted. 'Find something most normal people like and Tim
has a reason for not liking it. Wogs work too hard and make
everybody else look bad. Dogs piss everywhere and leave a
trail of hair. Kids are adults waiting to happen. You ka-pish,
Martinesi?'

'What about Ralph? Did Tim like Ralph?' We were running
now, the wind a whirl of litter and rain pelting fiercely
around us, thunder exploding overhead between sudden
bright cracks of forked lightning.

Somewhere a car skidded, but the numbing sound of
buckling metal never came. Dogs barked and the pavement
spat the rain back at us as we ran.

'Ralph wasn't a big topic of conversation in our house.
Besides, Ralph isn't any of Tim's business. Just because he's
screwing my mum doesn't mean he has to know every
bloody thing I do. Or everyone I hang out with.' There
was a touch of anguish in Nathan's voice. 'Mum and me
have a deal. She keeps Tim out of my hair, and I don't
bother him.'

We came to the warehouse finally and climbed through
our usual window to our corner. Soaked, we stripped to our
underdaks and lit a small fire from bits and pieces of old
wood offcuts and cardboard.

'Mum asked Tim to come along to Ralph's funeral,' Nathan
continued, 'but the prick said he was too busy. Doing what?
Who knows!'

'I guess not going to Ralph's funeral makes me a prick too
then,' I said defensively.

For a moment Nathan looked at me, then shook his head.

'I never said that, Martinesi,' he said. 'I've never questioned you about why you didn't show. You have your reasons.'

'And Tim doesn't? Get serious.' I sat down heavily. 'I just wish you'd say whatever it is you want to say about me not going to the funeral . . .'

Nathan laughed. 'Do you reckon you were missed, Martinesi? Is that what you think? Forget it pal, you weren't. No one gave a fuck whether you were there or not – '

'Except you,' I cut in.

Nathan sat down and stared into the fire, silent for some long minutes. I could almost see him thinking, his eyes twitching, his nostrils flaring. 'Martinesi,' he began finally, without a hint of anger, 'it's about time you took some responsibility for what you decide to do and stop justifying everything against what you think me or anyone else might think. You didn't come to Ralph's funeral, okay, you had your reasons.'

'You don't believe that though, Nathan,' I challenged. 'You reckon I piked out by using my parents as an excuse for not going. Well, I guess you're right. There, I've admitted it. I didn't go to Ralph's funeral because I couldn't bring myself to admit I really gave a stuff about him. He was your friend, your mate. I just sort of hung around the two of you like a bad smell. Like some dopey puppy looking out for scraps. I had no right to be there, Nathan. I've heard my old man get really pissed off after funerals where he's run into people who were there for no reason other than that ages ago they might have once met whoever died. My dad says you have to earn the right to mourn someone.'

'You're talking shit, Martinesi,' Nathan laughed. 'You didn't come to the funeral because you knew your parents wouldn't have understood how a nice boy like you could have known someone like Ralph. Simple.'

I opened my mouth to protest but Nathan held up both

hands. 'Don't apologise, Martinesi. It's one of the things I guess I really like about you and your family, you all try to see the best in each another.'

I felt ashamed and vulnerable. It was as though Nathan had divined a truth about my family that I had never seen.

'How do you explain what's happened to my uncle then?' I asked, hoping to contradict Nathan. 'My Nonna and Uncle Sandro won't have a bar of him . . .'

'I'm talking about your parents and you, Martinesi,' Nathan said. After a moment, he added, 'I wish you had been at the funeral, Martinesi, I really do. But I don't hold it against you because in your place I would have done the same thing.'

We sat there in silence, save for the crackling of the wood in the fire. It was as though some wall had finally come down between Nathan and me, a wall that until then I'd only been lunging at half-heartedly.

In the pale firelight Nathan looked a pearly white, his red hair now part of the flames.

'So, what did the Big Ig have to say?' I asked to change the subject. I saw Nathan's thin grin of compliance flicker behind the veil of firelight.

'He said we can have a Year 10 social as long as someone responsible takes the initiative to organise a committee to oversee everything,' he replied flatly.

'And of course you nominated yourself.' I bowed my head in mock subservience as I spoke.

'No, I gave Brother Ig your name, Martinesi. I told him that you'd make a very good head of our new Year 10 Social Committee.' Nathan didn't look at me as he spoke, but his eyes darted about the fire with so little focus I knew they spied me anyway. Before I could protest Nathan pushed ahead. 'I told Brother Ig that I thought it should be a year-level social where we would invite girls from all the local Catholic schools – St Mary's, the die-hards at St Catherine's, the wombats down at St Agata's, and maybe even some of the better ones from Columbus College. I told the old Ig that the boys would benefit from a little social activity. You know, a chance to mix with the fairer sex and all that – especially the footy and aths boys as a break from training. I told him a social would be a great morale booster, a way of unifying year-level spirit, getting the best from the boys, uniting their energies. And I told him that David Martinesi was honest enough, respected enough, and competent enough to head the committee.'

Nathan lowered his voice. A group of considerably older guys had just crawled into the warehouse and stood in the opposite corner shaking off the rain.

'Brother Ig reckons a social would be a fabulous way of instilling into the boys some good old-fashioned pride in St Joe's,' Nathan continued. 'It might even wean out some of the homo element. But I couldn't tell him that. I mean, you know you hear all sorts of stories about the frustration that strangles the life of men like poor Brother Ig that – ' He chuckled and drew my thought with his eyes.

'You're not a homo are you, Martinesi?' he shrieked with comic horror. Then grabbing at his wet shirt he pretended to cover his near nakedness while gibbering, 'Now don't you look at me, do you hear? I won't have you fondling my hose, you beast, you fiend, you – you homo-erectus – '

When I didn't laugh with him Nathan prodded me playfully.

'Ah, don't be such a suck, Martinesi,' he teased. 'Fuck, you'd think I'd dobbed you in to be an altar boy. Although come to think of it, you wogs are good at being altar boys. It gives your mums something to talk about seeing as most of you aren't any bloody good at footy. Listen, don't worry, Martinesi, it'll work out great.' He suddenly put me in a tight but good-natured headlock and grated his enormous knuckles on my scalp. 'It'll be UNBELIEVABLE – A TOTAL BLAST!' he roared.

'Well, Martinesi, are you going to say something or just sit there like an overstuffed cushion and catch mozzies with your mouth?' Nathan jeered and stepped back.

I needed a few more minutes to catch my breath.

'Welsh,' I eventually said in a voice as authoritative as I could muster, 'if you want me to head this Social Committee I'll do it on the following conditions.' I swallowed. 'Firstly, I not only get to write the letters of invitation to the other schools, but I also get to sit in on any meetings held with the representatives of those schools. Secondly, I won't be used just as a convenient voice-box and model-student figurehead. I want to be a real part of the Committee. I want to be involved in every part of the planning, from arranging the venue and date, to choosing the type of music. And thirdly – ' I paused long enough to steel myself for what I had to say next. 'Thirdly, I want you to stop ignoring me at school.'

On the other side of the warehouse the new arrivals looked across at me. When they saw me look back at them they glanced away.

Nathan finally spoke but it was as if he was far away, his voice on the end of some distant and frayed line of communication that threatened to cut off at any instant.

'It's a good thing for you, Martinesi, I don't feel like shoving this length of wood up your arse,' he said, holding up a smouldering piece of broken packing-crate, 'otherwise you'd be a very sorry wog right now. As it is I can't be stuffed getting aggro. I'm just a little too tired for all that shit.' He poked at the fire with the length of wood, stirring the embers and rustling the sparks into a cloud that might have been angry wasps for all their combined fury.

Nothing more was said about the social that afternoon, but a few days later I found myself summoned before Nathan, Anderson and La Rocca. They had set up council for me in their 'office' – the shower-block corner of the middle-school toilet. Two of the gang guarded the entrance.

Being 'summoned' was nothing new to me, nor to anyone else in the school. It was standard procedure that if you weren't part of the inner circle of the elite, you could expect to be called before Nathan's self-elected council to turn over your homework, forge notes so that council members could skip Mass, provide smokes or whatever else they chose to demand.

'Going to council' was so common that no one bothered with whispers, guesses or questions – unless, of course, it was the chosen-one's first such excursion, and then a crowd was sure to form outside the 'council-chambers'. I'd been summoned so many times before – more often than not so my assignments could be copied – that I didn't even get the customary escort.

The council members were quietly waiting for me when I entered the toilet block, but only after Nathan waved me over to a spot on the bench next to him did the others look at me.

'Martinesi,' Nathan began, getting right down to business the moment my bum hit the wooden slats of the bench, 'we've agreed that you will be offered the rare – the very rare – privilege of being inducted as an honorary member of the council until the social's over. Since Brother Ig thinks you're the person most capable of writing and speaking in an intelligent manner to the other school social committees, this council has decided that you can do it as an honorary member of the council.'

They were a shrewd bunch, I told myself. Shrewd and clever. By having me as an honorary member, and promoting the fact, all the good work I did and the social's success would wash over them.

But there were benefits for me, too, in the council's declaration of intent, and when Nathan asked me what I thought I replied that I'd do my best to make the event a success. When he grinned I knew for certain Nathan had calculated the benefits to me even before I had.

'Martinesi,' Anderson started when directed to by Nathan. 'There are a few rules you'll have to stick to though. First one is that you give complete – and I mean complete – loyalty to the members of this council. And that means not ever telling anyone who we are.'

Anderson, who walked with a slight stoop and was too tall for every desk he'd ever occupied, pointed a long finger at me. 'Two. You will always make it clear that you act as part of a team. We don't want a geek like you getting all the glory, do we. And three, you have to pass a task of initiation which Nathan here will choose and supervise.' He leaned forward towards me and I saw the scar on his forehead from where, years earlier, he'd been bashed by a member of an opposing footy team for calling the guy a wimp.

When I grinned Nathan said, 'Wipe that stupid smile off your face, Martinesi.'

And that was it. Our meeting lasted no more than ten minutes.

'You on the uptake, Martinesi?' Anderson asked just as I was about to leave.

I nodded and then La Rocca spoke up. Tall, solidly built,

with tight ringlets of jet-black hair, La Rocca had the crowd-stopping looks guys my age would have traded their souls for. His voice was a disappointment though, for despite his athletic physique La Rocca was, like me, on the verge of a vocal metamorphosis, so that when he spoke his voice cracked without warning. But he was still intimidating.

'I'm gonna be straight with you, Martinesi,' he frowned. 'I ain't keen on no bookworm being a member of this council, honorary or otherwise. It ain't no secret I don't think this is a good idea. But I'll go with the flow as they say.' He paused long enough to jab me lightly in the chest and look me right in the eyes. 'But you better watch your back, Martinesi, 'cos I'll be watching you.'

16

It wasn't until just before the social that Nathan and I finally felt up to visiting the cemetery.

'I really should meet this Zio Paul of yours,' Nathan said when he'd finished setting the crude cross we'd made into the mound of earth that was Ralph's grave. 'You reckon he's such a great bloke that I'm sure the two of us would hit it off . . . Two great blokes and all.' Nathan was crouched, one hand on the simple white cross where he'd written 'RALPH' in black marker pen, the other poking at the dirt. 'I don't ever remember having an uncle, or an aunt for that matter. Seems like it's just been me and Mum for a while.'

'I don't know that it's such a good idea to go visit my uncle,' I replied, hoping Nathan was only kidding. 'I don't even know if he wants to see any of us right now.'

Nathan shrugged his shoulders. 'We could tell him we're just passing through and want to see his missus.' He winked at me. 'No, seriously though, I'd really like to see this bloke who's so important to you.'

Important? I was flustered momentarily. 'I never said he was important to me.'

'Didn't have to, Martinesi. It's obvious. And hey, it isn't something to be ashamed of. I mean, shit, I wish I'd had an uncle or someone like that to look up to before – ' He seemed to catch himself and he looked away, reaching for the hammer that lay across the grave.

'Ralph,' he read slowly as he got to his feet. 'Not a bad sort of name for someone like ... well, like Ralph I guess.'

We stood side by side, our shadows merging in a blur at the foot of Ralph's grave. I wanted to ask him to finish what he'd begun to say but I decided it was probably better not to. I realised there were things that were more meaningful without the burden of words.

Putting the cross in place had been Nathan's idea. We were supposed to have been at school, helping decorate the hall for the social but, as always, Nathan had had other plans. We'd made the cross out of offcuts Nathan had taken from the school's workshop, shaping and smoothing it until Nathan was satisfied we couldn't do any better. It was his idea that we get the cross up as soon as it was ready, so we'd gone over the back fence at school the moment the paint had dried.

When I'd asked if Ralph's father would mind us putting up the cross Nathan laughed. 'Where does the Easter Bunny leave your eggs, Martinesi?'

'I still don't feel right about not putting Ben's name on the cross,' I said. 'After all, they are buried here together.'

Nathan pulled himself to his full height and gave the top of the cross one final solid whack with the blunt end of the hammer. '*He's* not my concern, Martinesi. And I somehow don't reckon he's yours either. We got St Vinnie's to help out with burying him, now I reckon he's on his own.' Then he walked off, not even stopping to look back at his handiwork. I knelt down beside the grave.

'You would have liked my uncle,' I found myself saying. 'He's a good bloke. Bit of a rebel, not really brainy, but pretty cool.' I realised with a twinge of guilt that I'd never thanked Ralph properly for having saved my neck on the silos. Was it really only a few months ago? I looked down at the grave.

'Zio Paul would have liked you, Ralph,' I whispered, and crossed myself the way Nonna said showed respect for the dead. 'He probably would have gone out on that silo for a mate too. He's like that.'

As I walked away from Ralph's grave I finally understood why Ralph had intervened when Nathan had been on the verge of pulping my face; in his way he was as much a stay-at-home as I'd ever been.

'So, you taking me to meet your uncle or what?' Nathan asked as I pulled alongside.

'My dad would skin me alive if he found out I'd been within shouting distance of the place.'

'In case someone sees you and starts a rumour about the family I bet.' Nathan's tone wasn't challenging and he added, 'I can understand that I guess. It would piss him off to think his son had gone behind his back, right? You Italians really hold to this family comes first caper, don't you? I mean, even if my old man was living at home and all, I don't think I could give a shit about how he felt about anything. But then, he never gave a shit about me either . . .'

'You never know,' I replied as convincingly as I could. 'Maybe if things had been different between your folks you might have felt different about your dad.'

Nathan laughed. 'The old man couldn't have been any different, Martinesi.' We stepped up to a tap to rinse our hands. 'My old man is the kind of person you don't want to get to know too well. He's what you might call a parasite.

When he walked out on me, Martinesi, I was a baby so I didn't know jack-shit about dads and mums and rellos and so on. I grew up without my dad – pretty much like your uncle. But when I started to see other kids with their old man, saw kids with two parents rather than one, you know what, Martinesi, you know what I felt? . . . I felt only half loved. Only half accepted, half wanted . . . Don't misunderstand, Martinesi, I mean, my mum loved me, still does and all, but . . .'

Nathan stood rubbing the back of his neck as though massaging a thought he wasn't sure about sharing. He stood like that so long I thought he'd finished, and I started to walk away because I didn't know what to say.

'Martinesi,' he called at my back and waited until I faced him. 'You've got no idea what it's like to be hated by your own father. And you know, I'm real glad about that. Real glad.'

'If you really want to, Nathan, I guess we could drop in on my uncle for just a minute,' I said, despite my certainty that in time the news would get back to my parents.

Nathan shook his head. 'You're right, Martinesi,' he said, pinching the tip of his nose. 'I reckon if I had an old man I could look up to I'd try hard not to disappoint him too.'

I almost made the mistake of telling Nathan that I knew just how he felt and that everything would be fine. Just in time I realised that I had absolutely no idea how he felt, none at all. My father might have been difficult to get close to, difficult to reason with at times, but my father didn't hate me. My father hadn't walked out on me. My father, for all his faults, tried hard to keep the family united, or at least together. In his eyes, to his way of thinking, there was family or there was anarchy. I could see that now. Yes, I could see that much.

I was, I had to admit, luckier than most. Despite all the restrictions. Despite all the weird and often embarrassing rituals left over from a culture that was mine only through inheritance, I was pretty fortunate.

'What do you reckon Ralph's doing right now, Martinesi?' Nathan asked suddenly, leading the way back out onto the street.

I shrugged, uncomfortable with the thought. 'Dunno.'

'You reckon there's a Heaven?'

'Nonna says there is. So does Mum. I guess . . . I guess I don't know for sure.'

Nathan sprinted across the road and I had to run to catch up with him. 'I thought it was part of you from birth, Martinesi, this believing in God and Heaven,' Nathan said as I caught up with him. 'I always reckoned people like you sort of grew up having some inner knowledge about religion and stuff, like it was just a part of you, you know.'

'Ralph's probably . . .' I searched for words to finish what I wanted to say, that Ralph was somewhere better than he'd been, but it all seemed so false and contrived, so instead I said, 'I'm glad I came along.'

Nathan grinned and narrowed his eyes. 'I reckon you are too, Martinesi. I reckon you are too.'

Later that day Brother Ig called Nathan out before the whole school and praised him for his exceptional leadership in getting the social organised. I ought to have been surprised but I wasn't. Nor was I surprised or angry that I wasn't called forward for individual recognition.

But La Rocca wasn't impressed with Nathan's public recognition and he made a point of telling anyone who would listen that the social was as much his effort as Nathan's, and that Brother Ig loved to play favourites.

'You're becoming a bit soft, Welsh,' La Rocca said when Nathan and I went into the hall after assembly to help with the setting up. 'Sucking up to Ig like that, it's just not like you. Well, maybe not like the old you anyway.'

La Rocca was standing on the low stage at the front of the hall directing some of the juniors on how they should pin up the posters. Nathan walked up to him, me in tow.

'It's never been a problem with you before, La Roc,' Nathan said slowly when he was at the foot of the stage. 'You never gave a shit about having Ig or anyone else praise you publicly. Why now? I thought getting a root was the main concern in your desperate little life.'

'See what I mean?' La Rocca said, knowing that everyone in the hall was listening. 'Get a life, Welsh. Ever since this social was brought up you ... you've been hogging the limelight.'

Nathan grinned and looked at me, eyebrows raised dangerously.

'You're a moron, La Rocca,' he said thickly. 'You're so full of your own shit that one day you're going to wake up and find yourself drowning in it.'

'So says the arse-licker himself – '

They were the only words he got out before Nathan leapt up, grabbed him at arm's length and shook him violently.

'Wake up to yourself, you deadshit,' Nathan spat, his face glowing red. 'You don't mean a thing in this place. You're a fucking loser. A loser, La Rocca. You reckon Brother Ig doesn't know that all this is just shit, eh? You reckon he doesn't know about you and me, and the council, and whatever other shit-kicking, no-hope, pointless piece of mindless theatre goes on around him. Who do you reckon pulls the strings that makes puppets like you dance, La Rocca?' Nathan fought to keep La Rocca from punching him. When one stray fist did connect with Nathan's forehead he dropped La Rocca with two quick jabs to the small of the back.

'There!' he shouted, standing over a stunned La Rocca. 'There's your share of the recognition. Don't let anyone ever say that Nathan Welsh wanted all the glory for himself.' Then back into the stunned crowd of onlookers he added, 'My name's Nathan Welsh, and that's a fact, even if Brother Ig never even knew I existed, you got that.'

'You're an arse-hole, Welsh,' La Rocca blustered as he got to his feet unsteadily. 'You and your bum-licking pet Martinesi, you're both arse-holes. Some day, Welsh, you're gonna pay for this . . . See if you don't.'

Nathan ignored him, but I saw the furtive glance he threw over his shoulder that confirmed what I'd worked out for myself those past weeks: the council was as much a con job as was Brother Ig's pretentious adherence to sporting glory and tradition. It was all a trick without mirrors, yet just as effective for those on the outside looking in. They were only shadows, whose greatest power lay in the intimidation created out of their unknown quantities. Once the unknown quantity was recognised for what it was, though, the intimidation disappeared.

'You're a dickhead, Welsh,' La Rocca sneered, staying clear of Nathan.

'Yeah, well, it's just as well we've all got you to look up to then, isn't it.' Nathan's voice was ice-cold, and he waited until La Rocca had slouched off cursing under his breath before turning on the onlookers, who seemed to wither under his snarl. 'Playtime's over! Get the fuck back to work.'

As quickly as it had erupted, the explosion was over. I followed Nathan through the unlocked door at the back of the hall into the tuckshop.

'I thought you guys never publicly disagreed with one another,' I said, 'especially not in front of us mere mortals.'

Nathan helped himself to a handful of lollies and I did too.

'La Rocca's the arse-hole,' Nathan said slowly, round a mouthful. 'He's got no discipline, no restraint.'

'So why d'you bother keeping him on the council?'

'There ain't no such thing as a closed circle. No such thing. The trick is to keep the ring as close to closed as possible,' Nathan mused. 'Dickheads like La Rocca haven't a clue about shit, and that's why they do what they do, why they self-destruct and by default – '

'Destroy the group,' I finished for him.

'Exactly,' Nathan nodded. 'You're catching on, Martinesi. I'm proud.'

I still couldn't understand why Nathan didn't move to have La Rocca kicked out, or at the very least censored by the other councillors, and I told him so.

'I wasn't going to tell you this just yet, Martinesi,' Nathan began, 'but I guess you should know before anyone else does, including Brother Ig. I won't be back next term. Come the Easter break that's it for me, I'm off, heading north – '

'Wha – ?' My mouth forced the word, mangled as it was, past my shock. Surely I'd heard wrong.

'Tim asked Mum to marry him back round the end of October and she's accepted,' Nathan continued, his eyes averted, leaning now against the wall where the tuckshop assistants hung the lunch orders. He took a long, deliberate gulp from his soft drink. 'Tim wants to take Mum up to Queensland – Cairns way – where he comes from originally.' He shrugged. 'If Mum goes, I guess I go, eh.'

I could feel despair creeping up on me again.

It was like Ralph all over again.

'You're bullshitting me.'

'I was going to tell you after the social,' Nathan went on. 'Had it kinda planned in my mind just how I'd do it too.' He sniggered self-reproachingly. 'Sort of like planning how to tell a girl you don't want to go steady any more, only harder, much harder, you know.'

No, I didn't know. I didn't know at all. I had absolutely no idea what it was like to break up with a girl.

'If you'd been listening real careful to me, Martinesi,' Nathan continued, moving to a spot against the wall directly opposite me, 'you might have figured it out for yourself.'

My mind stumbled over half-remembered conversations. Was he lying, or had I just overlooked the clues? I couldn't be sure.

I couldn't be sure. And then it occurred to me.

Late October.

Late October.

Nathan had known about the shift north *before* we'd ever made moves to becoming mates, certainly well before he introduced me to Ralph.

I looked up suddenly and the recognition of thoughts shared was there in that instant.

'Why d'you think I wanted you and Ralph to become friends, Martinesi?' Nathan asked. 'I wanted to leave Ralph with someone I could trust to care enough about him as a mate to want to look out for him. Someone who gives a shit about the world, about getting ahead. Someone with a bit of self-respect . . .'

Nathan's voice trailed off into an awkward silence. I couldn't take my eyes off him.

'FUCK YOU!' The words hit Nathan, making him jump. 'You fucking phoney bastard. You bloody phoney – '

There were words. I knew there were words behind the

ash in my head, the ash that now wanted to smother me, but they didn't come. The words were lost in the sudden pain.

Nathan blocked my way. I pushed at him. He staggered but came back at me, demanding that I hear him out. 'You're a lying bastard,' I snarled. 'You fucking use people to get what you want you – you – '

'Listen you stupid wog,' he said, grabbing me roughly. 'I'll admit that sure, at first I just wanted to be certain Ralph had someone to cling to, someone he could turn to when I'd gone. Yeah, and maybe it was a really selfish thing to do. But you've got to understand that you weren't just picked out of the blue you know . . . I studied you for months.'

STUDIED ME? . . . STUDIED . . . ME!

'What was I?' I scoffed. 'A rat in some fucking experiment?' Nathan ignored me.

'I studied everything I could about you,' he went on in the same thick tone. 'Where you lived. Who you hung out with. How many brothers and sisters you had. Whether you were any different at home to what you were like at school. Even how often you took the trouble to visit your grandmother – '

I prised an arm free and almost managed to grab Nathan by the belt before he pinned me again.

'Doing a thesis were you?' I said coldly. 'A study on wogs for your fucking graduation – '

'Yeah, you could say that,' Nathan cut in. 'I guess I was doing my homework. I guess I was trying to make sure that when I'd left, Ralph had someone to look out for him. Think about it you empty-headed fuckwit. Why of all the people I might have chosen did I choose you, eh?'

'To give me the shits,' I said, but the heart had gone out of my protest.

Nathan stepped back. He ran his hands through his hair and stared up at the ceiling.

'Yeah, you're right, Martinesi,' he whispered. 'You're right. I did everything I did just to give you the shits, just so Nathan Welsh could give David Martinesi the shits.' He looked down at me. 'But I guess Ralph got the better of both of us by getting himself barbecued, eh.'

17

'But Rosa is such a beautiful girl,' Nonna said yet again through the door of the toilet where I'd gone to try and get away from her. 'You would look so lovely at this dance together. You think I was happy when my brothers wouldn't take me to the harvest dance?'

'This is Australia, Nonna. And this is a social,' I called back in English. 'Maybe back in the old country brothers took their sisters to dances, but here in Australia we don't take sisters to socials.'

'What, you think I don't know this is Australia,' Nonna called through the door, then made her farting noise. 'I can't forget that this is Australia. How can I forget, you tell me. How?'

'Yeah, well, anyway, this is Australia, and I'm not taking my sister to the social, okay.'

Nonna was persistent. 'In one month Rosa will be fourteen. When I was fourteen I already had three men in their twenties lined up to have my hand in marriage. In this country girls like Rosa still think about dolls.'

'Rose sold her Barbies at the school fete last year, and

bought a broomstick with the profit,' I cried back and snapped the magazine in my hand loudly, hoping Nonna would take the hint and go away.

'You would enjoy the dance a lot more with Rose there at your side. When you arrive your friends will think how lucky you are to have such a beautiful girl on your arm, and the other girls will be jealous.'

'My friends would throw up!' I said and threw the door open.

That Rose herself didn't want to go, and wouldn't have been allowed to anyway, didn't seem to persuade Nonna otherwise.

Finally, though, Mum told Nonna to mind her own business, and I was able to escape to my bedroom. For well over an hour I circled my clothes, unable to decide what to wear, despite the fact that in the week leading up to the social I'd spent at least an hour a night sorting through my not-so-extensive wardrobe scrutinising everything from jocks to socks.

When Rose waltzed in I turned and raised my eyebrows as much as to say that her opinion wasn't needed thank you. But Rose didn't offer one; instead she sat on the end of my bed and watched in silence while I finished collecting my odds and ends.

'To your approval?' I asked casually.

'Chris and I broke up,' Rose announced matter-of-factly, one hand playing absentmindedly with the corner of my bedspread. 'And not because he's a Greek, Big Brother.' She paused and looked up at me, her eyes limpid and cool, her face set in defiance, 'His loss I reckon.' Rose's smile, when it came, was pained and I didn't know what to say, so for a few moments we said nothing. 'Why is it all the good-looking guys have to be so dumb?' Rose asked finally. 'I mean, Chris is handsome and all but he has no idea what to say or do around me so he does what comes natural to all animals: he gropes.'

I shifted my weight nervously. Hearing about my little sister being groped got under my skin. Rose noticed and added that the Golden Greek hadn't got anywhere.

'I reckon that's why he left me no choice but to dump him,' she snapped, suddenly seething. 'The guy's a walking, talking reason for contraception. I ought to arrange for him to meet the Pope, and whoever it is that runs their religion these days.'

'I'm sorry,' I mumbled before Rose jumped down my throat.

'Don't you feel sorry for me, David Martinesi. Don't you ever feel sorry for me. It's that Greek dick who's missing out.' Rose made a show of jutting out her chin and turning up her nose. 'I'm the Flower remember. Fiore, that's me. Zio Paul always said no one would ever be good enough for the Martinesi Flower.' She laughed at her own silliness then whispered, 'I wish he'd come back.'

'Chris?' I asked.

'Nah, stuff Christos. I mean Zio Paul,' Rose said. 'I don't know. It just seems that everything's too serious without him around. Have you noticed how Nonna hardly laughs any more?'

'What? Are you saying the walking stand-up comic herself is no longer bursting at the seams with hilarity? Oh, no ... it's the end of the world,' I said. I didn't feel up to a deep and meaningful right then. 'You've got it some problem wit moi?' I mimicked.

'I kind of miss being a kid,' Rose said with deliberate slowness. 'A real kid I mean, like when we used to hang out for Nonna to bring us her special boiled lollies. Remember those? Or how about when we got to collect gifts at the

Christmas party Dad's workplace put on every year. Remember how we'd fight for the tickets to the rides?'

'Yes,' I said as Rose got to her feet and adjusted my shirt collar.

Through a thin smile she said, 'Even if he never comes back I hope he's happy doing whatever it is he wants to do.'

I remembered. I remembered too what I'd told Nathan about how I loved Rose but had never actually told her. She was my sister, and brothers and sisters were meant to fight and bitch and argue with one another. Mum and her brothers argued – often. Dad and Zio Frank had had their moments. But ultimately it was all harmless – or was it? I wondered whether Zio Sandro and Zio Paul could or would ever reconcile their differences. And I wasn't so sure any more. They might tolerate each other, might even look back one day and laugh about what had happened, but the hurt and pain were real enough. They killed off something deep inside, something brittle and delicate called unconditional love.

'I just wanted you to know about me and Chris,' Rose said softly, one hand on the door knob. 'You know, I used to tell Zio Paul all my little secrets, and he never once let one slip. He was good like that.'

She was right. Zio Paul was good like that. But I hadn't known that Rose had confided in him too. And now Rose had shared something very important to her with me. That too was good. It felt good.

'Hey,' I called after her. 'Not all good-looking guys are dumb.' I did a twirl and bowed with an exaggerated wave of my hands.

'Yeah, right,' Rose laughed.

'Are you okay? About splitting up with Chris I mean?' I wanted to know. I really wanted to know.

Rose shrugged her shoulders, 'I guess there's plenty of other nice Greek boys out there when I'm ready.'

'Good one, Rose,' I said. 'Why don't you just put an ad in the paper calling for applicants: "Good Italian girl seeks nice, rich Greek doctor with own BMW for long-term family feud. Personal applications only. Contact very understanding Southern Italian father for more details and an interview to go over your bank balance." What do you reckon, Sis?'

'I reckon you're a bit soft in the head, David Martinesi,' Rose snapped back, but there was no anger in her voice and she closed the door with a shake of her head.

'*Mi sembri un Mafioso,*' Nonna spat when I entered the kitchen. 'Does he look like the sort of boy a nice girl would want to take home to his mother, I ask you,' she said.

'I don't think Davide wants to have a *nice* girl take him home,' my father surprised me with, from where he sat nursing his after-dinner short black laced with home-made grappa.

'You see, you see ... How can a boy grow up to be a decent man when he hears that sort of talk.' Nonna shook her hand at Dad but he only grinned at me.

'When I was your age, the last thing I wanted was for a nice girl to ask me back to her house after the harvest dance,' he added heartily. 'I didn't want to meet her parents.'

'Marco, please,' Mum cut in. 'You have a daughter too.'

'Rose is fine,' Dad pronounced with a wave of his cup. 'She has your temperament, Teresa. And you've got more balls than most men.'

Nonna made one of her fart noises just then and Mum shook her fist at Dad. But Dad was in a good mood and he just smiled sheepishly.

Rose smirked and made a point of ignoring Dad. 'Nonna's

right though, David. You do look like Dellavecchia.' When Dad didn't respond she went on, 'I tell you what though, if you were two feet taller, a lot slimmer *and* better looking, you could pass for a very young pre-flab Elvis.' She laughed.

Dad said that I looked like something only the police would pick up, but I think it was meant to be a joke because he laughed so hard he coughed up part of his dinner.

As always Mum came to the rescue. 'I think he looks very handsome.' It was something she always said, no matter what I looked like, even when I was the most awkward-looking kid in the school photo. She was standing beside me when she said it, and she reached out and touched me lightly on the hand, enough to let me know just how proud she was of me at that moment, whether for the way I looked, or because she knew just how hard I'd worked in organising the social, I wasn't sure.

'Marco, take your son to him social,' she directed, for there was no way I was going to be permitted to walk to or from the social in the dark. Mum waited for Dad to get to his feet before adding, 'You dance tonight, you unnerstand.'

'Not with a girl, surely,' Rose joked, and a moment later she grinned and told me that actually I did look okay even though my haircut was still daggy.

'Yeah, right,' I said, embarrassed at the attention.

Rose shrugged her shoulders and smiled as she admonished me, 'Better not break too many hearts, Big Brother, or you'll have me to answer to, okay.'

I looked at Rose. Her eyes were rimmed with tears but she hid them well, 'Okay,' was all I could think to reply.

'I think it's wrong that you don't take Rosa,' Nonna tried one last time when I gave her a goodbye kiss. 'Three men wanted to marry me at her age. Three, not one! And here my grandson won't even take his sister to a dance.' She pushed me away gently and narrowed her eyes. 'I will never understand this country,' she said.

'Tell you what, Nonna,' Rose said in Italian, borrowing the tone our mother used when she wanted to pacify us, 'maybe you can chat amongst your friends and find one who has a rich grandson of their own they want to marry off, what do you think?' She persuaded Nonna to be led back to the bedroom they were sharing, saying 'I want to hear all about the three men who wanted to marry you when you were my age.'

As Mum stood at the front gate to watch me get into the car with Dad, she gave me a little wave that seemed to take all her energy. I waved back, suddenly afraid of what I might be about to put myself through: I'd never danced with any girl save Rose or the odd family friend. It was almost a relief when Dad drove off and I knew there could be no turning back.

I knew I wasn't the only one feeling apprehensive about the social. After our confrontation in the tuckshop that afternoon Nathan, who'd disappeared for two hours, returned just as I was locking up the hall. He'd handed me one of two identical gold and black lapel badges, worked into the shape of a clenched fist. Nathan explained that it was the symbol he and Ralph had planned to use on the back of matching leather jackets they had dreamed of owning.

'It's something Ralph and me talked about, you know,' Nathan had said as I'd listened with a feigned lack of interest. 'I guess it really stands for all the questions me and Ralph have ever asked ourselves.' Questions, he'd gone on, like: Why, if there was a God, had He or She allowed Ralph's mum to die and his uncaring, alcoholic father to live? Or, how come Ben always got on better with their father than Ralph did? Why did Ralph have to sometimes sleep outside when his father brought a woman home for the night while Ben got to sleep at a friend's? Was there really a father for every child born, or was it better to forget and pretend that sometimes there wasn't?

In my own mind I added another one: Why, if you find someone you think can be a true friend, do you always have to lose them – and perhaps more than once?

Nathan hadn't apologised for what had happened in the tuckshop, but he'd insisted on my wearing the badge. 'I'd like you to wear this tonight, Martinesi,' he'd told me without ceremony.

When I'd asked where he'd got them Nathan had replied that the badge he'd given me had been Ralph's. 'I found it amongst Ralph's things when I went round to his place to tidy up a bit, you know. I . . . I reckon he'd want you to have it now.'

I put the badge on the moment Dad turned the car into the school grounds.

'Here's fine thanks, Papa,' I said and almost leapt out while the car was still in motion.

'*Aspetta*. Just a minute, wait.' My father nosed the car towards the cyclone fence and switched off the engine.

For a long minute he didn't say a word. He just looked at me, his eyes huge for a change, veiled with other thoughts, other concerns.

'I gotta go, Papa,' I said.

He reached over and tapped me lightly on the forehead. 'This you got good, Davide,' Dad said through a grin. 'You brain is clever. You are smart. You have much intelligence in you head. Maibe too much.' He paused and patted himself on the chest. 'For this I is glad. Proud. Much thanks to the God for you cleverness. But – ' He drew a breath that seemed to swell him to bursting. 'But, but . . . But a big brain, much intelligence, much knowing of dis and dat is of no use if a man sees fear in every shadow, even his own. A man has a brain to serve him in his life, not a life to serve his brain. You unnerstand what I'm saying, Davide?'

We were parked with our backs to the hall, and the pale lights that surrounded it cast dark shapes where we sat. Yet I could see my father clearly, perhaps more clearly than ever before. His words were alien to me, though. As unnecessary as my trying to explain to him why I'd never be like him, why I'd never be able to fulfil his every expectation, his every dream for me. He knew, and I knew that. I didn't even need to tell him about having seen him in Fernando's, nor ask him why he was there. There are things, I realised, between a son and his father that need no words. Like the regret Nathan felt for never having known his own father. There were no words needed to express that. It just was. The question of Fernando's was just one such question. My father going there, it was just a part of his life, not mine. Not unless he wanted to tell me about it himself. And for now he didn't

'Yeah, I understand, Papa,' I replied. 'You can't be a slave to your brain – '

'To yourself,' Dad corrected me. 'You must not be a slave to yourself.'

I didn't know what to say and fidgeted with the door instead.

'*Sei fatto grande ormai*,' Dad added after a few moments. 'You grow up so quick I not can believe was so long past you was run round look for me all time.' He paused. 'All the time you was follow Papa,' he added, 'I not even can go toilet without you was there wait for me. Is like yesterday when you was born. But was not.' Dad put out his hand

181

and shook mine briefly. 'I hope you hiave a good time tonight.'

I felt lucky to have my father sitting there, overworked and tired, and disappointed by much of what life had dealt him, yet content in his own way. I felt lucky and glad to have my father wish me a good time.

And I felt Ralph at my back as I stepped away from the car and watched my father head out towards the road. Not a ghostly apparition of Ralph, not some woo-woo spook Ralph-come-back-from-the-grave, but a living, breathing, thankful Ralph who shared in my gladness as much for himself as for me.

When I looked round Nathan was standing there.

'You ready, Martinesi, or what?' he asked, the badge on his shirt collar catching the light as he turned for the hall, where a crowd had already gathered.

For a moment I hesitated, having half-expected to turn and find Ralph looking over my shoulder.

'He's a good man, my dad,' I said at Nathan's back, the words spilling from me as though in affirmation of something I must always have known. These were the words I had wanted to say to my dad only a few moments earlier. It was as though I was defending my dad against the images of Nathan's dad and Ralph's dad, men with whom I could never imagine my own dad ever having sympathies.

We were just short of the hall when Nathan stopped and waited for me to come alongside. I noticed how much older than me he looked now that he had spruced himself up, the air around him sharp with aftershave.

I realised how much I'd miss Nathan once he'd gone, and the incongruity of that thought when I remembered how scared of him I'd been only a few months before made me chuckle out loud.

'You right there, Martinesi?' Nathan grinned.

'Yeah, yeah I'm fine, Welsh,' I replied, and this time it was me who put an arm around his shoulder. 'But I've got to ask you something, something Ralph told me that I've always meant to ask you about. Do you really go to Mass every Saturday night with your mum?'

Nathan glanced towards the hall. 'Why do you ask?'

I shook my head. It was another of those questions to which I already knew the answer, but I wanted Nathan to confirm it for me.

'It's the only thing Mum ever asks me to do,' Nathan replied. 'Don't you ever do something just because someone asks you to?'

18

For two whole days after the event the social was *the* topic of conversation for all the Year 10s. La Rocca had kept his distance during the night, and continued to do so afterwards, but the other council members were more forthcoming. There were pats on the back all round, and even a handshake from Brother Ig for each of us involved in organising the night.

I was thinking about how proud I'd felt at that moment when there was a short rap on my bedroom door. My mother stepped into the room. When she drew back the curtains and flooded the room with stark late morning light I became aware of someone else standing in the doorway to my bedroom.

'Nathan?' I said, sitting bolt upright. It was the first time Nathan had ever been in our house, let alone my bedroom. Nathan looked down at the crisscross pattern of the vinyl floor and remained silent as my mother opened the window, collected my discarded clothes and carefully selected my clothes for that day.

'It's all right, Ma,' I said, waving her off, eager for her to stop embarrassing me.

'Wot, you fren never see clean clothes before,' my mother laughed, waving her hand dismissively.

'Ma,' I protested, 'please – pl-ease.'

'Well,' my mother said, 'I hiave much work to do.' Then to Nathan, 'You like stai for lunch?'

Nathan's head snapped to attention and he looked quickly over at me. My mother had never even met him before.

'Nathan and me have got things to do,' I piped up. 'I – I guess I forgot to tell you, sorry.' I feigned a quick glance at the clock on my side-table, alongside my model Ferrari and plastic Spitfire, things that seemed out of place now that Nathan was in my room. I was certain he didn't have toy cars, model aeroplanes or a bookshelf crammed with junk.

'I didn't realise it was so late, mate,' I said with too much emphasis. 'Sorry you had to come over and call me – '

My mother opened the door and leaned close to Nathan, a smile across her face. 'If you two finish you bisnis on time, Davide's Nonna she make tagliatelle. You welcome join with us.' Then to me, 'No need you be shame of you family, Davide.' She closed the door with a slow wink that left me groping for a reply.

'Cute room,' Nathan said with exaggerated relish.

I followed his gaze as it passed over my childhood mementoes; the carefully arranged rows of Matchbox cars on my dresser, the plastic soldiers huddled in two neat and opposing ranks on the bottom shelf of my bookcase, the stuffed toys piled into a basket by my desk, and Superman and Batman comics gathering dust in a box by my wardrobe.

'Mum doesn't like to throw anything out,' I said. 'I – um – I'm thinking of painting my room soon and ... and then shifting all this junk out.' I shrugged my shoulders hopefully and wished I'd been able to intercept Nathan at the front gate.

'So, you seemed to enjoy having Rita's tongue in your mouth for most of the other night,' Nathan smirked when he spotted the scrap of paper on which I'd scribbled the phone number of the girl I'd spent most of the social with. 'I told you I'd fix it sweet for you to get to meet her didn't I.' That was true. After I'd confided to him that Rita had caught my eye, Nathan somehow managed to get us together. He had embellished my reputation, telling Rita that I was captain of the school's soccer team, and who was I to have contradicted him!

'Yeah, well, thanks for that,' I mumbled. 'She's a nice girl.' Thank God she hadn't been 'nice', I thought. Two inexperienced kissers would've been one too many.

Nathan rolled his eyes and stared at me. 'Rita DePietro can't spell the word, Martinesi, or are you brain dead from the waist down?'

'We didn't – ' I started but stopped when Nathan laughed.

'What didn't you, Martinesi?' Nathan smirked. 'From what I saw I reckon it got pretty heated under that altar-boy skin of yours ...' He paused and fingered the scrap of paper, holding it out gingerly in my direction. 'I reckon all that Italian red-blooded passion that you'd been bottling up since kindergarten came surging through the other night. I mean poor Rita looked stuffed by the end of it, and I've got to tell you, Rita DePietro's got stamina, mate. But a word of advice, just don't show too much interest, Martinesi, or you'll have her looking elsewhere for kicks, know what I mean?'

I snatched the number from Nathan and dropped it into the top drawer of my desk. Rita DePietro could wait. And so could I. 'Yeah, well, she wanted me to have her number,' I said by way of explanation, and crossed to the door as though to convince myself it was shut.

'Well, this is a surprise,' I said. 'You've never – '

'Been here before,' Nathan finished for me. 'You never invited me, Martinesi.'

I looked hard at Nathan then glanced away quickly. 'Guess I never thought about it. Sorry.'

Nathan plonked himself on the end of my bed and threw his arms up, 'Hey, it's no big deal. I mean, I never expected you to, you know.'

We were silent then, the two of us.

Nathan broke the silence. 'The cops came by my place about an hour ago. They wanted to know whether I could maybe tell them why Ralph and his half-brother were inside the workshop the night of the fire.' On the shelf above my bed there was a photo of Rose and me at Phillip Island, on the beach at Cowes, and Nathan fingered the edges of it as he spoke. 'They said I'm the only friend they can conclusively link to Ralph, except for some kid Ben's old gang couldn't remember the name of, except by an odd nickname – Flat-arse or something.'

Nathan stopped fingering the photograph and looked up at me.

'Don't worry, they won't come here. The cops I mean,' he continued. 'I told them that Ralph didn't have any other friends, that he lived a pretty sheltered kind of life. As for why he might have been at the workshop, I told them I didn't have a clue. They suggested robbery.'

'And?'

'And – and I told them Ralph wouldn't have understood the idea of burglary, let alone attempted one. And you know what, Martinesi, I really believe that. Whatever reason Ralph had for being in there with Ben and Tag, it wasn't burglary. No, I reckon Ralph just wanted to do something to win Ben's approval.'

Nathan picked up a copy of the book I'd started reading before I'd ever met Ralph, a book I hadn't touched much since. He turned it over absentmindedly then looked back at me.

'Seems strange, doesn't it? That Ralph would have wanted to be accepted by Ben even after all the shit that Ben put on him. All the crap he gave Ralph including that stuff at the warehouse. But then Ralph wasn't your average kind of guy, was he? You didn't always know for sure what was going on inside that head of his. Even when you thought you knew him, Ralph could spring a surprise on you. Like he did back at the silos that day, remember?' Nathan gave a nervous chuckle and shook his head. 'Bloody idiot he was sometimes. Problem was, of course, that Ben thought Ralph was more an embarrassment to be endured than a brother to – ' He dropped the book on its spine.

I finished the sentence for him. 'To look after.'

'Ralph just wanted a brother, you know,' Nathan went on. 'Sometimes you just want someone you can talk to, you know, about – things . . .'

Somewhere down the hallway outside my door Rose's voice announced that they would be late for Mass if Nonna didn't hurry up.

'You wanna borrow Rose?' I quipped in an effort to break the awkwardness.

Whatever it was that Nathan and Ralph had shared, it went beyond friendship – and I had to accept that for Nathan, at least for now, no one and nothing could replace Ralph.

If we were anything, I told myself that morning as Nathan sat on the edge of my bed and waited for me to dress, he and I were the missing pieces to each other's jigsaw-puzzle lives. Ralph was the shadow at both our backs, as much a part of our lives dead as he had become while alive.

'It's all right to say you love someone,' I found myself whispering, my arm gentle on Nathan's shoulder, my father's voice in one ear as I spoke the very words I had so often heard him utter in comfort to others. Not for the first time I found myself wishing I'd had the nerve to say as much to Rose when she'd opened up to me about her and Chris splitting up. And to Zio Paul as well.

I felt Nathan stiffen, his neck grow taut. His head was bowed and he was breathing steadily. My mind groped for something more substantial to say but failed. For me to say that I too loved Ralph would have been stretching the truth. I didn't love Ralph, at least not in the way I loved Rose or Zio Paul, or –

Or, if I was honest with myself, the way I loved Nathan – with a strong desire to be like them and to have them count me amongst their most valued friends, to have them turn to me for support.

What I wanted . . . what I wanted was for them to rely on me the way I'd come to rely on them. I wanted them, and Nathan in particular, to feel empty at my absence in the same way I felt theirs when they failed to be there for me as I'd come to expect. Yes, even Nathan Welsh.

I wanted to be an important part of their lives, the way Ralph had come to be for Nathan, the way Nathan had come to be for me. I was, I suddenly realised, jealous of what Ralph and Nathan had shared and continued to share. This was the longing I'd felt in the warehouse. This was the longing of only a few minutes before: the longing to mean as much to Nathan as Ralph did.

It was a selfish desire. But there was no denying it any longer.

'You still got that key I gave you, Martinesi?' Nathan's

question pierced my mental fog. I nodded and he added, 'Get it.' When I hesitated he said more forcefully, 'The key, Martinesi, get it now, I need it.'

Not wanting to lose the key Nathan had given me, I'd dropped it into an empty football-shaped piggy-bank and was able to retrieve it quickly. I also reached for the badge we'd taken to wearing out of school hours.

'You want to come over for lunch like Mum asked?' I said for something to say. But Nathan didn't bother replying, although I doubt he'd heard what I'd said, for the moment the key was in his hand he was out of my room with a quick 'C'mon' thrown over his shoulder.

I barely had time to yell down the hallway that I'd be back soon, before Nathan was hurrying out the front gate, leaving me to chase after him as he broke into a brisk jog through the park and then along the road leading past the silos.

All the while I ran after him Nathan never once looked back to see if I was following. Even when he cut from one block to another by short-cutting over fences Nathan didn't pause for me. He just ran on and on.

And I ran with him, tight-chested, muddle-minded and only vaguely aware of where we were heading. Running because I knew I had to.

19

The house Ralph had shared with his father and half-brother was a dump. Resting on blocks of wood, it was a fibro-sheet knock-together with a flat roof of galvanised iron. It sat isolated on a block overgrown with weeds and littered with rubbish, and the toilet was a ramshackle thing down the back.

'Welcome to Hell,' Nathan shouted when I caught up with him on the footpath outside the house. Then he was over the low wire fence and charging up the few steps onto the veranda, which had collapsed and was hanging loose, like the tongue from a strung-up corpse.

A moment later the key he'd taken back from me was in the lock and the front door yawned open with faint murmurs of protest.

Why, I asked myself, had Nathan given me the key to Ralph's house? 'What are we doing here?' I called through the open door, trying not to sound perturbed.

There was no answer so I crossed the veranda and peered inside. The stench engulfed me and I recoiled to the crumbling rails that ran almost the length of the rotted veranda.

'You coming in or what, Martinesi?' Nathan was at the door leaning out towards me.

'It stinks!' I complained.

'A lot of things do,' Nathan replied, then he was gone from sight again.

As I turned to go inside I saw the word 'Hellsville' scrawled on the wall near the door.

'Ben's little joke,' Nathan explained when he saw me looking at it. 'Very imaginative don't you think? Or what about this one?' He ushered me inside, like some curator of a backwater museum no one ever visits. He read the graffiti that covered every surface of the room in a loud, booming voice, as though he wanted the world to hear him. Cops are pigs, Dope dupes dopes, Satan rules where God ignores, Every day is Friday 13th, Castrate Abo's and all other animals, Suck more piss, Glory equals dying young, Ben woz ere, Shoot up, don't give up.

But for two mismatched couches, a low coffee table, and sheer muslin curtains at the window, this first room was bare. At least I thought it was until, pushing one of the couches aside, Nathan revealed a chest of the kind my own parents might have packed their few belongings into when setting out for their 'new' life.

'Ralph's wardrobe,' Nathan announced curtly, then pointing to the couch closest to the window added, 'Ralph's bed.'

Nathan was pushing me towards another room. This one opened up off the first room and was pitch black until Nathan reached for the light switch. I soon saw why; a wardrobe had been pulled across the window, blocking out any natural light. Above me a single naked bulb hung on the end of a long black cord, its glow a muted apparition that barely illuminated the single bed against one wall, its blankets heaped on the floor beside it.

'The lion's den,' Nathan growled, and kicked at a pile of yellowed newspapers in the centre of the room.

From this room we passed into the kitchen. It contained nothing other than an old gas stove, a cupboard, a black bar-fridge and a round table with four unmatched chairs.

Nathan crossed the room and plunged his hand into the free-standing sink, fishing about and holding out to me a plate on which food scraps had sprouted slimy mould.

'The dishwasher died some time ago,' he said sarcastically, 'and good help is so hard to find don't you know.'

'And this,' Nathan declared as he led me into the last and smallest room, his arms thrown wide as though to embrace it, '*this* is the utility room ... For guests perhaps. Maybe a visiting relative ... A long lost son.' His laughter exploded through the room and I had to steady myself.

'This isn't funny, Nathan,' I managed to get out.

'Funny no, hilarious YES,' Nathan spat back. 'Can't you just picture Ralph sitting here to a lovingly prepared meal of home-made pasta or a leg of the juiciest ham? Perhaps a glass or three of home-made vino, eh? Wot you tink paesan!' He sat down heavily in one of the chairs and slouched across the filthy table. 'And when dinner him finish, we just sit back and watchit the televish.'

Nathan bolted out of the chair and crossed the space between us in two strides.

'No, it isn't funny, Mr Martinesi,' he agreed in a whisper, 'but it is real ... All this shit is as real as Ralph himself was ... is ...'

I blinked into the silence. 'You took a chance coming here, didn't you?'

Nathan feigned fear. 'OH NO, THE OLD MAN! Where is the old bastard? Oh God, he might be here! He might be – in the oven – in the cupboard – what about under the table?'

And he looked in each of these places before catapulting out the back door.

'C'mon, Martinesi!' he cried, 'we might find him in the dunny having a shit.'

I was saddened by the sight of Nathan tearing about the back yard like a dog off its lead, running around and around the toilet calling out, 'The old man's coming! The old man's coming!' until he exhausted himself. Then he sat down amongst the weeds near the back steps and stared at me as I stood by the door.

Nathan waited for me to sit down too, before saying softly, 'You're probably wondering why I gave you the key to this place, eh. Guess I'm just a mad prick,' he laughed.

'Why *did* you give me that key?' I asked.

Nathan used the tip of his cigarette to light another for me. I took it reluctantly.

'Because this is the key to the real world,' he whispered. 'I wanted to leave you a note telling you to use it to go have a look at this if you had the balls.'

'Why?'

Nathan shrugged. 'I was pissed off at you for living the way you do – as though it were your fault.'

The cigarette smoked in my fingers.

'I don't get it,' I said feebly.

'You haven't got a clue have you, Martinesi,' he laughed. 'You haven't got a fucking clue in the fucking world.'

'Listen, mate,' I snapped back, 'if you're going to talk crap I'd rather you kept your mouth shut, you know.' I got up as though to leave but Nathan grabbed me.

'Just sit down, Martinesi,' he said repeatedly until I sat myself down on the step above him.

'Martinesi,' he began once he'd finished his smoke. 'Martinesi, you've never once asked why I promised Ralph's mum I'd watch out for him, have you? And you've never questioned why I'd rather hang out with Ralph than La Rocca, Kosta or any of the others. I mean, I've told you what I think about school and our council, but you've never asked me why I'd spend my time with someone like Ralph. Or you for that matter.'

'Do what you like Welsh. You always do.'

Nathan laughed again. 'My mum said that to me when I told her I wouldn't go up North with her and Tim. "Do what you like," she said, "just stop being a selfish little bastard and think about someone other than yourself for a change." I had to laugh didn't I? What else could I do? After Ralph I mean. After I'd spent almost every day since his mum died doing my best to look out for him.'

'So tell me,' I said stiffly, 'why did you take so much interest in Ralph? And why'd you have a key to this place? And what was I supposed to do with it anyway?'

Nathan got up suddenly and went inside. By the time I got to the front room he was crouched at the chest that had been Ralph's wardrobe. He was looking for something, digging through the bundle of clothes, shoes and a few carpentry tools. I went and stood behind him, looking over his shoulder.

'You know, Martinesi, the cops took a lot of shit out of this place,' Nathan explained as he foraged. 'That morning after Ralph and Ben died, and I came back here, the cops tried to get the old man to tell them if there was anything here that might help them with their investigation. I mean, look around at these walls. You'd reckon the cops could've figured out from all this crap that Ben wasn't exactly an Einstein. Just what did they need for their investigation, a taped confession that yes, Ben and Tag had gone to Gaglieri's to rip him off?'

He found something and began unwrapping it, asking me to sit down. 'Maybe *you* still believe in the tooth-fairy, gold at the end of rainbows and gingerbread men, Martinesi.' He shook his head slowly and then handed me what he'd been looking for.

'What is it?' I asked.

'Aladdin's lamp.' Nathan snorted. 'You do know a photo when you see one don't you?'

Nathan knew that wasn't what I'd meant.

I stared for a long time at the framed black and white photograph of a quite handsome man, mid-thirties perhaps, dressed in a plain open-necked shirt and stove-pipe trousers, hair combed up high over his forehead. He was holding a child – a boy, I judged, from his clothes – over one shoulder and smiling proudly.

'Ralph?' I said, pointing at the child. Nathan nodded. 'So I guess this must be his dad.'

'Good work, Sherlock,' Nathan grinned. 'Now, look at this one,' he said, and passed me a photo he'd taken from his wallet.

This photograph too was of a man and a child, again a boy. Only this photograph was a grainy colour snap, and the man in it was perhaps a few years older than the one in the first photograph.

I looked back and forth from one photo to the other. The men in both shots had a similar stance: legs slightly apart, back arched away from the camera, head cocked to the left. I suddenly realised that I was looking at two photographs of the same man taken a few years apart, and I looked up at Nathan.

He reached out and lifted the colour photo from my hands. 'I was a cute kid wasn't I?' he said dryly. 'Not as cute as Ralph there, I'll admit that much, but not bad for a red-head.' He paused to let what he'd said sink in. 'My mum was just as stunned as you are now, Martinesi, when I showed her this.' He put the photo back in his wallet. 'She thought she'd hidden it well enough. Well, did I surprise her, eh.'

He laughed under his breath. 'It took her a while but she finally admitted that my old man had indeed come home once, for a short time. A sort of "Let's try again" phase but it hadn't worked out. The photograph's a memento I guess.

'That's Ralph all right there in *that* photograph. And that's my dad – his dad. *Our* dad.' A laugh died in his throat. 'The real funny part is that by the time I was born, the old man already had Ralph. Seems he was getting a little bit on the side, on the sly, you understand, and Ralph was the booby prize.

'Funnier still, Martinesi, is the fact that my mum and Ralph's mum were best friends. My dad was screwing my mum's best friend, and until about a year and a bit ago she didn't have a clue, not a fucking eye-blinking clue.' He paused and fixed me with his gaze. 'You see, Martinesi, some families start out wrong and get progressively worse. But if the old man had just not come back into our lives maybe ... maybe things would've turned out different for Ralph – and Ben.' After a slow breath he added, 'For me even.'

Nathan began to throw Ralph's clothes around, tossing them in all directions at once, losing himself in them as he went on. 'But no, after being away for years and years, the old bloke turns up on Shelley's doorstep – Shell's, that was Ralph's mum – and begs forgiveness. Up until then Shells had never said a word to Mum about who Ralph's dad was. She blamed it on a pub floor root while she was pissed.

'And for all those years I played with Ralph because he

was my mum's best friend's kid. We were both *only* kids. We had that much in common you know, that we were fatherless.' Nathan raised his voice a little and asked, 'Do you want to know what it's like to be fatherless, Martinesi? It was worse for Ralph because he couldn't quite grasp the idea, you know.

'But I'd grown up around Ralph and I'd got to know his ways, so that whenever he wanted to know about this father business I'd tell him we were the lucky ones, not those poor kids with dads at home to kick them around when mum had had enough.'

Nathan stopped talking and sat down on the coffee table. 'Try to imagine my mum's reaction when the old man suddenly rolls up out of the blue *and* moves in with her best friend. You reckon the shit didn't fly!' He shook his head. 'I'll say this much for him, the old man must've been a smoothie to convince Shells to give him a go. I mean he'd already failed with Mum, so I guess he figured Shells was his last hope. Until Shells got real crook that is.'

Nathan lit another cigarette. It was a few minutes before he went on, and I just sat where I was, conscious of a weight that sat in the pit of my stomach.

'Friendship's a funny thing, Martinesi. I know because I saw how it got to Mum after Shells became too sick to care for Ralph – and Ben, who was in the picture as well by then, but I won't go into that now. Fuck no, too confusing. The sicker Shells got, the more often Mum went to see her. Always, of course, when the old man wasn't in. I mean, it makes sense now doesn't it, why Mum seemed to have no time for "Shelley's friend", but back then I just never gave it much thought. Oldies are always shifting and changing their loyalties. But as Shells got more and more sick, Mum did more and more for her, especially since "Shelley's friend" never seemed to have time for much besides drinking.

'As for me and Ralph, we just went on pretty much as always, despite Ben. I figured Ben for a dickhead right from the start anyway, and maybe that's why I tended to close in more and more around Ralph. I sorta knew, even then, before I knew any of what I'm telling you now, that neither Ben or the old man was going to bring any good to Ralph. And they didn't did they.'

'I don't know if you've ever watched someone die, Martinesi,' Nathan went on. 'You know, I can remember the smell of Shells as she was dying. Strange that. But anyway, about a week before she actually died Shells asked to see Ralph. And that's when she told him who this bloke she'd claimed was "just a friend" really was. And who Ben was. And you know what? Poor Ralph didn't quite know what to do or say. He sort of just wandered around not really appreciating what his old lady had told him. "I got a dad?" he'd ask over and over.

'There wasn't any need to tell Ralph,' Nathan continued after rubbing his eyes with the palms of his hands, kneading them into their orbits. 'What the fuck was Ralph gonna do with a dad like that, Martinesi, you tell me? What difference did it make to Ralph after all those years to be told, "Hey kid, meet your old man."?

'Of course Shells never told Ralph the entire story. Not the additional little detail about how his old man was my old man too. Nah. In fact she never even told me, not even after I'd shown her that photo of the old man and me.' Nathan lowered his voice to just above a whisper. 'She must've known though. Shells must have known that it wouldn't take long for me to find out. Not after she gave Ralph that photo you're holding, knowing full well about this one.' He tapped his wallet. 'I don't know how many times I showed Shells that shot of me and the old man after Mum had told her about how I'd come across it, about how relieved she felt that at least that much of the past was in the open.

'Mum would say, "Just a glimpse of the past is more than enough, don't you think, Shells love." Makes sense now. Poor Shells, how hard it must have been to sit there, look at that photograph and have to bite her tongue, knowing what she knew. What a thing to have to live with. No wonder she didn't want to carry it with her into the grave.'

If Nathan had expected me to say something he was a long time waiting. Nothing coherent came to my mind, my thoughts awash with a numbing sense of alienation, vulnerability. My hands fell between my knees, shaking, unable to orchestrate even a mimed response.

'I used to curse Shells for telling Ralph the truth you know,' Nathan went on while I remained speechless. 'I mean you'd think she could have left it alone. When I first found out about the old bloke being Ralph's dad I was really pissed off. I was angry for Ralph. I could've killed that bloke for having walked out on his son,' Nathan laughed, 'the way my old man had walked out on me. Can you believe that? I was angry at this bloke because *my* dad had walked out on me, and then I discover that *this* bloke *is* my dad – and Ralph's my half-brother. And Ben ...' Nathan tossed his cigarette aside and shut his eyes a moment, squeezing them tightly.

'You know what I reckon, Martinesi,' he said, his voice rising, 'I reckon Shells told Ralph herself because she probably figured the old bastard would eventually tell him himself.

'I've never told anyone this before, Martinesi,' Nathan whispered as he carefully, methodically began rewrapping the framed photo. 'The day I put all the pieces together I went over and tried to bash the crap out of the old man. I belted him over the head with the biggest lump of wood I could find. I just smashed that friggin thing across his fucking skull and then ran like all fuck out of there.'

Nathan stopped and took a breath, rubbed a hand across his face. 'Three whole fucking days of my life wasted crying over something I couldn't ever change. But you see Martinesi, I was scared shitless. Scared that I'd killed the fucking mongrel. Not that he might be dead, no. I was scared I might be put away. I was scared my mum wouldn't want to know me any more . . . I was just so shit scared.'

It was then that Nathan looked directly at me and I saw that he was crying.

'He didn't die of course,' he whispered, 'and I was found eventually and brought back. The real surprise though was that the old man never laid any charges. He told the cops that he couldn't remember exactly what had happened, that he never saw anyone and that I had run away because we'd had a disagreement a few hours before, and that it was just coincidence about what happened.

'I don't know if they swallowed it all, but the fact is I got away with it. It was Mum who paid some price for all those lies though. As sure as I'm talking to you now, Martinesi, I know in my heart that Mum somehow made it sweet for me with the old man and the cops.'

Nathan finished wrapping the photo and got to his feet. 'You asked me not long ago about why I go to Mass with my mum. I guess now you know. Before this business about going up North, it was the only thing she'd ever asked me to do against my will. I don't believe in God, or Heaven, or even Hell. Not the way you do, Martinesi. But I do believe that sometimes you've got to give a bit of yourself to someone else, even when it doesn't particularly suit you.'

'So now you know, Martinesi,' he grinned after a moment of silence. 'Now you know the whole story. The why and the who and the how.'

My legs were so wobbly Nathan had to steady me towards the door. He helped me onto the veranda then pulled the door shut behind us, pocketing the key.

'I was going to let you find that photograph for yourself,' he explained as we walked in the shadow of the house towards the front gate. 'I was going to leave a note explaining where you could find it, what to look for, leave a few clues for you to sort through.'

I felt giddy and didn't respond, trying my best just to keep up with Nathan, who seemed to be in a hurry to put some distance between us and the house where Ralph had tried to live.

'That offer to have lunch at your place still on, Martinesi?' he asked when we'd reached the main road.

We were standing on the tram tracks, cars on either side of us, the traffic of people going about their late-morning business. I stood rubbing my temples.

'Yeah, of course the offer still stands,' I replied finally.

20

All the way home I wondered whether or not to tell Mum and Dad about what I'd seen and what Nathan had told me. I wanted them to know about the sort of life Ralph had lived. They'd probably known a Ralph or two in their own lives. And yet they had made me feel as though I couldn't even mention Ralph to them. No one had a right to deny anyone the right to know that there was more than one way to live a life.

But in the end, as I stood and watched my mother at the kitchen sink, and stirred the sauce as she'd asked me to, I decided I wouldn't mention anything about Ralph at all. It would be my secret. Mine and Nathan's. I was David Angelo Martinesi, and not Marco Martinesi or Teresa Martinesi – or even Rose Martinesi. I wasn't any of them, but they were all part of me.

When I'd finished with the pasta sauce and turned to the table I saw that it had been set with the blue tablecloth my mother only ever used on very special occasions.

I tried an off-hand chuckle. 'What's all this, Ma? I mean, it's only Nathan.'

She ignored my question and said instead, her native drawl slow and measured, 'Go call your papa. Your Nonna and Rosa will be back from church soon and I want everyone *here* to eat at one time.' Then she added, 'If you don't hurry, Davide, my sauce will overcook, the roast will dry out and the lettuce will go limp.'

That's when I counted the two, rather than one, extra settings.

'There's one too many,' I told her. 'Unless you're expecting Dellavecchia.'

'You're right,' my mother shot back. 'There always has been one too many. From the day your papa arrived here there has always been one too many. But today it will stop. Today all obligations will be satisfied.'

'Ma?'

'Tell your papa to come home,' she went on, her eyes on the simmering sauce. 'Tell him . . . Tell him, Teresa Martinesi desires the company of her family at lunch.'

'Nathan'll think we run a restaurant when he sees this set-up!' I joked, but I avoided looking at my mother. 'He'll get the wrong idea about us, Ma. He'll think we're loaded – rich. He'll think all that stuff they hear about us wogs, us Italians and Greeks and that, having four houses, a block of units, an acre of land in the middle of nowhere where we grow marijuana – he'll think it's all true.'

When I stopped and looked at Mum she was frowning in my direction. 'I'll put Nonna's tagliatelle on in fifteen minutes,' she announced, then jerked her chin towards the door. 'You might need to run.'

I was going to ask, 'Run? Where to?' but realised the answer was there in the tone of her voice.

Outside it was unusually warm. The air I gulped as I ran full pelt to Fernando's was like molten metal in my throat.

Mum had known about Fernando's all along! And if she knew *that* about Dad, what else would she know?

Outside Fernando's I stopped to catch my breath, walking right past the men at their tables and Fernando himself at the bar, past a group of kids shouting obscenities at one another around the billiard table Nathan and I had lost to Ben and Tag on, and through the door marked 'Private. No you go inside unless nok first!'

'Papa,' I began, trying not to show the fear that gnawed at my bones or the sheer exhilaration of the moment. 'Papa, the Signora Teresa Martinesi desires the company of her family at lunch without delay.'

There was a deafening silence. And in my rush to crash through the door I hadn't noticed Fernando yelling at me to stop. 'WHAT YOU DO, EH? WHAT DO, YOU BLOODY IDIOTA!?'

He was strong for a man well over sixty, and I found myself being hurled against the billiard table when a second voice called out.

'*BASTA!* STOP!'

'Fernando, you fat donkey. Is that the way you treat my godson?' Dellavecchia was already walking towards me when Fernando began apologising, straightening my clothes and generally back-pedalling.

'Get the boy a drink – *after* you apologise properly to him,' Dellavecchia went on and, putting an arm around me, he led me to a table at the front of the café, adding, 'I'm sure the boy has a very good reason for going where he has no business going.'

I had never particularly liked Dellavecchia before, but as of that moment I loathed him. I knew that Mum expected me to make sure Dad brought Dellavecchia home with him but I shrugged free and walked quickly back towards where my dad stood in the doorway amongst a group of men that included Mr Valdo.

Everyone was watching me now, and there was absolutely no doubt in my mind what Nathan would have done in my place.

My father was stern-faced, his eyes cold. He was ashamed of me. I had humiliated him.

'Mama asked me to come call you to lunch, Papa. She's got everything ready, including the blue tablecloth, and she'd like us all to sit down together.' I glanced over my shoulder at my godfather. He was leaning against the bar stirring a short black Fernando must have made him as a peace offering. 'Mama says Signor Dellavecchia's invited too, if he'd like to come.'

I turned and walked out.

I walked out without looking left or right, or back into the crowd of men who were whispering amongst themselves.

I'd done what I'd done. Tingles of dread and excitement peppered my arms, back and legs as I started towards home, my breathing strained.

Nathan's voice weaved in and out between every gulp for air. *Don't you ever do something just because someone asks you to?*

All the time, I thought, I've always done my best to . . . to do what everyone else expects me to.

I slowed down. That was the point, wasn't it? That there's a difference between doing something for someone because you want to, and doing something simply because you're expected to.

Ever since I could remember, Giuseppe Dellavecchia had been there in the background, with his wealth, his power and his dubious credibility. But my mother had always seen it for what it was, a total fake.

It was all a con. Nathan had exposed it for what it was: a con by those who are scared over the ones they want to intimidate. So Dad had lived a life of obligation, trying to pay back to that prick Dellavecchia a debt that never really existed. He'd been used by Dellavecchia, doing what Dellavecchia had come to expect of him, simply being there when Dellavecchia wanted him to be.

But there wasn't time to give much thought to all this because when I got to the back gate I realised Nathan had beaten me home. Not only that, he was chatting away to Nonna over by the hen-hatch, a large paper bag in his hand.

When I got closer I noticed something else about Nathan Welsh. He'd changed out of his jeans and baggy shirt into trousers and a crew-neck T-shirt complete with breast pocket, and he'd given his fly-away hair a solid brushing. And there was something more, something like the sense of pride I felt at having been made a part of the world, scarred as it was, that Nathan and Ralph had shared.

'G'day, Martinesi,' he said breezily when I approached. 'Your Nanna – Nonna, sorry – your Nonna here, was just filling me in about her hens.' He grinned like a kid who'd been offered an icy-pole on a hot day. 'Did you know her favourite hen, Con . . . Concetta, is probably the oldest hen in Australia. Isn't that so, Nonna?'

Nonna, who spoke English the way I speak Mandarin or Japanese, kept nodding her head while Nathan spoke. When I asked her if she'd been boring Nathan with tales about her wondrous 'two-dozen-a-day' hens, Nonna beamed one of her generous why-do-you-ask smiles and told me my friend was very interested.

'You didn't understand a thing she said, Welsh,' I chided him. 'Don't you know it's cruel to fool an old lady?'

'Better that than ignore her, eh,' Nathan shot back. 'Besides,

I got the gist of what she said. I mean, all you wo – all you Italians speak using these fancy hand movements.' He waved his arms wildly, 'Pretty soon we Skips pick up on the intent. Ka-pish?'

'You been here long?' I asked as I led Nathan back towards the house, he winking at my Nonna, who giggled back behind her crumpled hand. 'And why all dressed up?'

Nathan did a curt spin, 'You like 'em, eh. I just thought, you know, it's my first time with the future in-laws and all – '

I looked hard at Nathan.

'What? What'd I say?' he spluttered innocently.

'In-laws my arse, Welsh,' I laughed. 'My sister's going to marry a doctor – or at the very least a lawyer – the *word* according to my mum.'

'Who said anything about your sister, you cute wog boy you.' And Nathan pinched my cheeks, exactly the way Zio Paul liked to do when he was teasing me. 'Come 'ere and give us a kiss.'

'You're such a – a – ' I began but let the sentence go. 'About before,' I said after a moment. 'At Ralph's place. I – '

Nathan quickly put a hand up to silence me. 'No more about that okay,' he said sharply. 'I've come here to have lunch with my mate and his family, and that's all. So just let it rest, okay?'

21

From the moment Dad waltzed in for lunch with Mr Valdo instead of Dellavecchia, all conversation around the lunch table stopped. Even Nonna, who seemed to want to talk for ever to Nathan about her hens, lost interest in what she'd been saying and tried to concentrate on not chewing with her mouth open.

It was Nathan who finally broke the silence. 'So,' he said chirpily when there was no more food to devour, 'you must all be pretty proud of David here.' He was looking from my mum to my dad and back again, one hand resting lightly on my shoulder.

Rose frowned and her eyes darted from me to Nathan and then to Mum and Dad. 'About what?' she asked.

Nathan let his hand drop and straightened his back. 'Oh,' he whistled through pressed lips. He turned to me, 'You mean you haven't told your folks yet? And here I was thinking this was a celebration lunch. I mean, you know, if I'd been asked to be a representative on the School Council I – well, I guess I would have blabbed it to everyone.'

I was caught off guard. What the heck was Nathan going on about?

'Are you telling me, Mrs Martinesi, that David hasn't mentioned that Brother Ignatius wants him to be the representative for the Year 10s on the very important, you know, School Council?'

'Davide?' my mother prodded.

'Cose'e successo? Wa hiappen?' Nonna asked looking around for someone to explain.

'My brother on the School Council,' trilled Rose. 'You gotta be joking?'

My father looked on. Here at last was some promising news, a possible breakthrough for the Martinesi clan.

I kicked Nathan under the table.

'Oww,' Nathan protested with mock seriousness, 'I'm sorry . . . I mean, I thought you would have told everyone by now.'

'Davide?' my mother tried again.

Bloody Nathan, I thought.

'Go on, Martinesi,' Nathan encouraged. 'Seeing as I've already spilt the beans, you might as well tell them about Brother Ignatius being so pleased with the way you conducted yourself over the school social that he called you into his office on Friday – ' Nathan faced my father, 'and asked you to consider being the Year 10 rep. Go on, tell them.' And Nathan smiled at me, but not in the way he might have done a few months before if he'd set me up.

I swallowed.

'I bet you must be really proud of your son, eh, Mr Martinesi?' Nathan said to my dad. 'I reckon if I had a dad, a real dad I mean, I reckon he'd be as proud of me as I bet you are of my mate here.'

I stared down at my hands.

Nathan's words bounced around in my head. Whether what he'd said was true or not wasn't the issue. Whether I could find the courage to quit apologising for what I'd done was. At least to me.

Then slowly, his words chosen carefully, my father spoke. 'When I comes to this country,' he began, 'I had not more than the shoes on my feets, and the suitcase I carry on the ship. I doan hiave mother, father, brother, sister . . . No hunkles, hunties . . . Like much of them what comes before me I not got much for myself. What I got is a dream to make better my life. To make better the life of my family which I leaved behind me. It was my duty, my responsibility to make money and send it back to my mother. She comes rely on me to send back to her some money what she can put aside for send herself and my brother here . . . To this country I telled them was too good, too beautiful, with so much space. Not like my village which got one tiny house lean against another one. Them look like toy house for doll, not for people.

'I was young man when I comes here,' he went on above my head, above all our heads as we sat there, only Nathan and my mum looking at him. 'I not shame who I am, because I know I comes here to make better myself and my family. But not everyone him know this so I was call lots names from many people what thinks I was coming here free charge. They think my voyage was paid by guverment to come to Australia and make myself rich man. But that not how was. Not 'tall. I comes here on money borrowed from someone else who can afford the cost, but not guverment. I never been got money from guverment. Not even I know what is be unemployed. I never not work all the time I been in this country.

'I work hard, day and night. Sometimes go straight one

211

job to another and no sleep. I live with three other young mens like me, together in a bungalow where we share three rooms. Not three bedrooms, but three rooms, one, two and three. Like me them too work for send money back to them family in Italy, money what can be use to feed them mother, father, brothers, sisters ... on and on.' Dad paused and coughed as though to clear his throat. 'With time me lucky enough find a good and strong woman who love me enough to come be my wife, and so slowly, slowly together we make something from nothing. But not easy to do this.'

I felt my father's shadow at my back, saw it lean lightly across the table. I swallowed, but couldn't say a word. I listened instead.

'When you young you believe only you can know the way to do this and dat. You think you so strong you can make the moon rise, the sun shine ... You think in you head dat in future you always hiave more than what you got. But you discover as older you grow that this not is always true. Sometimes what you got is everything you ever will hiave. And you need learn be happy with this, other sense you lose even dat. Today my son David, he came call me come lunch like I was him brother.'

I cringed, feeling his humiliation.

'He can do this because him young, him hiave eyes look forward not back, eyes for see where is that he can go, but maibe not enough where him comes from. And him decide him not going where I want him go, no ... But funny this is. I never say to him, you must this, you must that ... It is himself believe this 'bout me. Him confuse hope with expectation.'

I thought I heard my mother sigh, but it was Rose, staring right at me. I blinked once, hard, then looked back at the tablecloth, wishing Dad would stop. But he didn't. He had more to say and he was going to say it.

'I learn one thing about what it mean be a stranger, to be the one always looking in,' he continued, only now he stood behind his chair, hands resting on it lightly. 'I learn it is a good thing to lead rather than always to follow. I learn there is a time for both, to lead and to follow. You follow so to learn. This must be true or you just follow because you are lost, hopeless. But must come a time stop to follow and start to lead. This must be true too. And sometimes to lead is no easy, no easy 'tall. Sometimes to lead takes some guts and tough decisions, like tell an old man to wake up his-self and no be slave to his-self no more.'

Out of the corners of my eyes I saw my father coming round the table. No one moved. It was as if it was just Dad and me in the room at that moment. I concentrated on a splash of sauce on the blue tablecloth.

'Mr Nattam,' my father went on, 'David, him is a thinker, not joust a worker like him father, and this is very good. Of this, yes I am proud. Very proud.'

I almost expected my father to touch me, to lay a hand on my head the way he did when he wanted to put an end to a disagreement or misunderstanding. Instead he went outside, and Mr Valdo followed him a few moments later.

There was something in my eyes but it wasn't tears. Rose and Nonna, oblivious of what had taken place between my father and me, sat staring blankly at me.

'What was all that about?' Rose asked.

In Italian our mother said, 'Your papa has a few things to think about. I think it best we leave him alone with his thoughts for a while.'

Nonna, who, like Rose, hadn't grasped any of this, folded her arms across her chest and made her farting sound before

213

speculating that she and Rose were perhaps being taken for a ride.

Nonna and Rose left the table, on the pretence that Nonna needed Rose to help her sort through some odds and ends she no longer wanted to hoard, leaving Nathan, Mum and me sitting around the sacred blue tablecloth, each waiting for the other to speak.

Finally I decided there was no point in continuing all that crap about being a School Council rep any further. 'So what was all that meant to prove?' I hissed at Nathan, startling my mum.

At first Nathan didn't answer; he merely stared at the tablecloth and fiddled with a napkin, folding it into different shapes. When he did speak his voice was a bit jaded but under control.

'I guess I shouldn't have surprised you like that, Martinesi,' he said, no hint of apology evident in his tone. 'But I reckon you trust me enough to know I wouldn't bullshit to you in front of your folks about something like the School Council.' Then to my mother he added, 'For a smart kid your son's a bit of a thickhead, Mrs Martinesi. No offence to you – ' When he pushed his chair back my mother rose with him.

'Thanks for lunch,' Nathan said cordially. He patted his belly and observed, 'If I ate this good every day I reckon I'd be a real fat arse, Mrs Martinesi. It isn't every kid who's lucky enough to have a real family to sit down and pig out with.'

My mother smiled at this rather peculiar compliment and nodded her head appreciatively.

'You come enni time you like,' she announced. 'Always is enough food for frens.'

'I'd like that, Mrs Martinesi, but Mum, me and Mum's boyfriend Tim will be leaving earlier than expected. We're going up North, you see. Mum's boyfriend got word yesterday this job has come through, but he's got to start pretty much straight away, otherwise they might get someone else.'

Nathan knew I was watching him although he didn't shift his gaze off my mother. But he wasn't talking to her any more, not directly; he was talking to me.

'You mother hiave boyfren. Dat nice,' my mother observed. 'Dai get marry?'

Nathan smirked. 'I guess so, once we get properly settled. Tim reckons living up North will be good for Mum, and me as well. He's trying hard to get me an apprenticeship with a mate of his who runs a freight business, you know, moving stuff interstate in trucks. Tim says that since I'm not cut out for school he's willing to put a word in for me with this mate of his and see if I can't join his road crew, learn the ropes – '

'You not like school?'

'Put it this way, Mrs Martinesi,' Nathan laughed, 'I'm no doctor. I'm more what you might call an oil-and-grease man. Give me an engine and I can strip it bare and rebuild it for you. But give me a book – ' He shrugged his shoulders.

My mum drew her hands together and held them under her chin. I thought she was going to pray. 'I wish to you the good luck,' she smiled.

This time it was my turn to leave the table, and Nathan and I were almost across the park before he broke the silence.

'You'll be good on the Council,' he announced as though that were the uppermost thought on my mind.

'You could've told me,' I snapped.

'I apologised already.'

'You know what I mean.'

Nathan stopped and let me get a few strides ahead of him before he yelled at my back, 'Grow up, Martinesi. Stop being such a deadshit and crawl out of your fucking shell.'

When I turned to look at him he was standing rigid, one hand raised in my direction. 'Not everything goes according to some blueprint you might have all drawn up inside your high-IQ mind, Martinesi. Some things have a way of arriving unannounced. What did you want me to do, run over and tell you the moment Tim got the news?'

I stormed back to Nathan and growled right into his face. 'I expected you to treat me like a friend, Welsh! I expected you to tell me direct. That's what I expected. And that shit about the Council. What was that all about? Who were you trying to impress – my mum?'

Nathan blinked slowly, his eyes looking right through me, making me step back in surprise and fear.

'What you expected, Martinesi,' he began softly, 'was that whatever plans you made would be followed precisely. That's what you expected. And if you think about it, it makes no difference whether I leave now or in five weeks. You either learn to stand on your own two feet or you don't.

'Yeah, I went to see Brother Ig, but only after he called me into his office and wanted to know if he could count on you to have some balls when it matters. Well, maybe they weren't his exact words, but that was the gist of it.

'You see, Martinesi, it's pretty much like your old man said. You either follow so that you can learn to lead, or you follow because you know no better. You make up your own mind, Martinesi, but don't blame anyone but yourself. Ka-pish?'

Nathan pushed past me and I watched him walk away.

My head throbbed. I felt my body stiffen with anger and I shut my eyes and gritted my teeth against it.

Yet my anger was not directed at Nathan, or my dad, or my mum. It wasn't even directed at the things in my life that had always shadowed me: the tag of stay-at-home, being an outsider because my parents were caught between two cultures, not having the courage to stop being a victim of my own fears. My anger wasn't even directed at the other stay-at-homes who were probably just waiting for a Ralph, a Nathan, a chance of their own to see beyond the obvious. No, this was an anger without any one purpose or focus, it just *was* – and it flowed through me and out again as I watched the one person I'd never have imagined could have become my closest friend cross the road towards the silos.

It was a few minutes before I could bring myself to follow Nathan, but when I did and called out for him to wait up he ignored me. It was only when I scrambled up to the top of the silos that he finally turned to face me.

'Ralph and me always thought you pretty lucky to have your own garden, David Martinesi,' he said slowly. Then he turned and walked, nodding curtly down towards my house and its garden. 'I mean, you can grow your own vegies and stuff. And in summer you can just sit out here at night and water the plants and listen to the cicadas. We used to watch you sometimes, Martinesi, me and Ralph. From up here. We used to watch you and your old man cut and gut the chooks. We'd see you chase the headless chook about and kind of half die yourself when your old man told you to pick the bloodied corpse up and pluck it. Shit you were a funny sight, Martinesi.

'You had your own little private world behind that fence there. You and your old man I mean. It was sort of good, you know, to watch you and your old man doing stuff together in there where no one else – except us of course – could see. I often wondered what it'd feel like to have a back yard and some vegies and a few chooks to stir up. And a dad who'd take the time to teach you how to do things like kill a chook or dig the soil for the tomatoes – shit like that. Normal stuff. Everyday kind of stuff.'

To hear Nathan speak of that as 'everyday kind of stuff' made it all seem okay – acceptable even – for the first time in my life. 'Dad'll be getting ready to make the wine soon, why don't you come round?' I said impulsively. 'We can always use an extra pair of hands – or feet,' I laughed to myself.

I must have pulled a face, because Nathan laughed, too. Then he reached into the paper bag he carried, and held a small wooden object out to me.

'Here,' he said much more quietly, 'this is for you. I reckon Ralph would've wanted you to have it.'

As I looked at it, Nathan prised the carving out of my hands. 'This way up, you dork,' he said.

'What is it?' I asked.

'It's not finished,' Nathan whispered. 'Well – I – I sorta guess it *is* since you know, well, since Ralph ain't around to actually finish it properly. It's supposed to be a – '

I cut Nathan off with a wave of my hand. 'I'll guess,' I said. 'It's a penguin!' The object in my hand had suddenly taken a concrete shape. 'It's a penguin, see? See, that's the back of the head, and that's the curve of its back. And this,' I pointed to an odd protrusion at its base, 'this must be its tail, or whatever you wanna call it.'

I turned the carving over and over. 'Look there,' I went on, excited now. 'You can see where Ralph had made a start on the face . . .' I ran my palm over a water-smooth curve. 'You can tell he'd already started on the head from the way this curves here, see . . .' I turned back to Nathan. 'Thanks,' I whispered, 'but where'd you get it?'

'Ralph told me before I went away that he wanted to make something for his – quote – "new mate", meaning you,' Nathan explained. 'I guess it was his way of saying thanks for the sausage and everything.'

I looked up at Nathan, my eyes wide with surprise.

'Yeah,' he smiled back. 'It was me who suggested you might like something to remember your first real holiday by, so a penguin seemed just the thing, given that you were off to Phillip Island.'

'And the Penguin Rock Caravan Park,' I added.

'I knew he'd been working on it for you, and I knew where to find it, you know, after the fire and that. I was going to wait until just before I left to give it to you, but I figured as I was coming over for lunch it might be nice . . . right. It might be right to give it to you now.' Nathan shrugged and sat on the edge of the catwalk, his legs dangling free. 'Put it away somewhere safe, Martinesi. Never know when I might want to have another peek at it.'

I didn't know what to say, so I said nothing. I sat down beside Nathan, leaning forward against the railing so that I could peer down into my back yard.

In my hand was the unfinished carving Ralph had been making for me.

I knew then. I knew even as I sat there, even though I'd only known Ralph a very short time, that I owed it to myself as much as to Ralph never to forget what it was like to be a stay-at-home.

About the Author

Archimede Fusillo was born in Melbourne to Italian immigrants. Since completing a Bachelor of Arts and Honours in Psychology at the University of Melbourne he has worked as a teacher and as a features writer for two international magazines. Many of Archimede's short stories have been published in Australia's leading literary magazines and journals, and he is also the author of two textbooks.

Archimede lives with his wife and two young children in Melbourne.

MORE YOUNG ADULT FICTION FROM PENGUIN

Looking for Alibrandi   Melina Marchetta

Josephine Alibrandi feels she has a lot to bear – the poor scholarship kid in a wealthy Catholic school, torn between two cultures, and born out of wedlock. This is her final year of school, the year of emancipation. A superb book.

Winner of the 1993 CBC Book of the Year Award for Older Readers.
Winner of the 1993 Kids' Own Australian Literary Award (KOALA).
Winner of the 1993 Variety Club Young People's Talking Book of the Year Award.
Winner of the 1993 Australian Multicultural Children's Literature Award.

Johnny Hart's Heroes   David Metzenthen

Working as first-time drovers for Johnny Hart, Lal and Ralph find themselves inching along a dusty, desperate road. There is a future there to be grabbed if only they can outlast the drought, roll with the punches, absorb the knockbacks, and stick together. But nothing is easy in the nineties in the not-so-lucky country. Especially when the odds are stacked, and not in your favour.

Sleeping Dogs   Sonya Hartnett

The Willows are a dysfunctional family, and when one of the five children befriends an outsider who wants to uncover their secrets, the family's world is blown apart ... Another powerful and disturbing book from this talented young writer.

Winner of the 1996 Miles Franklin Inaugural Kathleen Mitchell Award
Winner of the 1996 Victorian Premier's Literary Award Shaeffer Pen Prize.
Honour Book in the 1996 CBC Awards.